Andrew Chalkley was bo   ⅃ѹ. After
completing a Geography d   ⅃ɕd to be a teacher,
and taught for nearly 30 yeaᴦ. ⅃⅃ schools across Hertfordshire
and Bedfordshire. This is his first novel.

For my nan,

Mabel Jean Hill (1918–2017)

Andrew Chalkley

TRAVELS WITH MY NAN

AUSTIN MACAULEY PUBLISHERS™

LONDON • CAMBRIDGE • NEW YORK • SHARJAH

A CIP catalogue record for this title is available from the British Library.

ISBN 9781786936950 (Paperback)
ISBN 9781786937711 (ePub e-book)

www.austinmacauley.com

First Published 2023
Austin Macauley Publishers Ltd®
1 Canada Square
Canary Wharf
London
E14 5AA

A big thank you to Hilary Wood, who provided invaluable advice and guidance along the way.

Synopsis

I always wanted to ask my 94-year-old grandmother what she did during the war...

On a warm spring day in 2012, two elderly sisters; Mabel and Di, sit side by side smiling, as they are about to toast the latter's one-hundredth birthday. Nobody present could have guessed that over 70 years ago in the early spring of 1940 Mabel's life hung in the balance, dependant on the actions of her older sister...

As an unwilling resident of Templars retirement home, 94-year-old Mabel Hill fills her time stirring up trouble for the unpopular manager Mrs Caunter. These antics are shared only with her favourite grandson, who wants to succeed where the rest of the family have failed, by finding out what she did during the Second World War.

The opportunity never seemed to arise though, until he drives her half way across England to attend her older sister's birthday celebrations. His quest to unlock the secrets of Nan's youth is about to begin...

Mabel will not yield her secrets that easily though, and her narrated memories first feature a shy schoolgirl growing up in the small Hertfordshire market town of Baldock in the late

1920s and early 30s. Subsequent outings or 'travels' follow, as visits to Mabel's old haunts bring back the fascinating and gripping exploits that epitomised her war, before one final emotional journey to France reveals a startling secret and the shocking truth…

Chapter 1

It's not very often you get invited to a one-hundredth birthday party, so the fact that I was to drive my Nan over 150 miles to celebrate her older sister's century was not much of a sacrifice to make. This was despite my ever-growing reluctance to venture out onto our increasingly congested and lawless roads. My family had deemed me the most suitable driver to provide Nan with the smoothest journey, allowing for the fact that she was 94 years old and suffering from osteoarthritis.

I couldn't help recalling the entertaining novel by Graham Greene, one of my favourite authors.

Like his narrator Henry, I was about to embark on my own travels – involving a modest hatchback rather than the Orient Express; a destination somewhat less glamorous than Istanbul or Paraguay (Gloucester); and a female companion even more elderly than Greene's Aunt Augusta.

This was my 94-year-old grandmother, Mabel. The single most noticeable character change that occurred in Nan as she aged was that she had lost any prior inhibitions about social etiquette, and would speak her mind most freely. Unfortunately, she was deaf in one ear and tended to speak loudly or even shout, so that the person being talked about (and sometimes subjected to barbed remarks) was often all too aware of what she had just said. This caused my mother and her two sisters a good deal of embarrassment, while the rest of the family laughed, and no doubt encouraged her further in her new-found role of retirement home comedienne.

Nan, still fiercely independent, had moved into Templars retirement home in Baldock three months earlier after another fall, her fourth in total. Faced with this option or a nursing home, she had very reluctantly and often ungratefully ceded ground to her three daughters. True to form, she would not let them forget about this and regularly played on their guilt. Nan was still mobile, and would use a walking stick or even a frame when she didn't think anybody was looking. Her daughters endured her criticism of their joint coercion, safe in the knowledge that anytime she did get into difficulty, help would be on hand from the staff.

At first Nan chose to stay in her room and requested room service at meal times, rather than eat in the communal dining area. However, her natural curiosity soon got the better of her, and more recently she had started eating with the other residents. This seemed to coincide with an upturn in her general health as, not wanting to be wasteful in front of others, she started to eat more.

Her recent falls had been caused by dehydration leading to dizzy spells. Now that she was eating more, she inevitably drank more too, especially since she piled mountains of salt on any food she ate. As someone who was born during World War I, grew up during the Great Depression and endured all the food shortages World War II brought, she was definitely not one for wastefulness. This was an enormous relief for the family, and worth battling Nan's long and determined resistance against leaving her own home.

I vividly recall helping her leave her house of 34 years, which had definitely become too large and difficult for her to manage. Even packing up Nan's belongings became a war of attrition, as she actually refused to say which items she wanted to keep and which she wanted to throw away or donate to charity. Therefore, it was a collective effort along with my sister, our mother and her two sisters to sort through nine decades worth of material. I remember thinking how bizarre is the amount of useless objects that we humans buy and collect in our lifetimes. Nan was certainly no exception.

The pile of pointless bric-a-brac was building up into a sizable mountain, with a miasma of styles from across the decades, including several pieces I had bought her for various birthday and Christmas presents. However, we all experienced the awful feeling that you were dismantling someone's life and merely consigning most of it to half a dozen black bin bags, never to be seen again.

The most interesting items that I sorted through were Nan's old black and white photos. These were not huge in number; Mum had always said money was tight. The sepia prints and their documentation of how rapidly social history evolved over the past century both intrigued and encouraged me to find out more about the life of Nan's generation. The photo of my Nan's wedding day to the one grandparent that I never met was one I had seen before, but I always studied it hard, trying to imagine just what he was like. Families tend not to ask each other about dead relatives, and ours was no exception. It was easy enough to ask who was in the picture, but too many personal questions proved difficult. As I flicked through the rest of the photos I would occasionally pause and ask Mum who certain individuals were.

On one occasion I came across an image of two young girls, which I assumed was my mother and one of her sisters. Mum corrected me when I checked with her, and pointed out that it was in fact Nan with her older sister Di, probably aged eight and 14 years respectively. Both girls had smiles that beamed out from the photograph and prompted me to ask Mum a question:

"Were they very close?"

I was referring to their childhood, since I knew that they very rarely saw each other these days. Living 150 miles apart prevented regular face-to-face meetings, but even so I could only recall meeting my great auntie Di on a handful of occasions.

"No, they barely see each other," Mum replied, not really listening carefully to what I was asking, and continuing to sort Nan's belongings.

"I meant when they were growing up."

"I don't think so, your Nan doesn't really talk about her. Di moved to Gloucester as soon as she was married."

Di's late husband came from Gloucester, and the couple had moved there to live with his family shortly after the marriage. Nan would have still been at school then, so I thought it must have been hard on her, effectively to lose a sister in her mid-teens. Assuming that Mum knew very little other information of interest, I put the photograph to one side and persevered with the sorting.

*

The morning of the expedition to Gloucester had arrived, a fine, warm and sunny April day. We travelled in a convoy of two cars from Mum's house to the retirement home, a trip lasting less than ten minutes. In total there were six of us making the journey, the other four (my parents, my sister and her six-year-old son) would be travelling in one car, while I drove Nan. Mum was always criticising Dad's driving as being erratic but she never volunteered to drive herself.

Having perhaps expected Nan to be prepared and ready to leave, I found her in the communal lounge looking fairly nonplussed.

"Have you forgotten then?" I enquired, making sure I was speaking to her left ear, knowing full well that she wouldn't hear me in the other one.

Nan raised her eyebrows and laughed, "Of course I haven't, I just thought I'd come in here and make some mischief."

I raised my eyebrows and grinned, knowing that her daughter would be here shortly and far from impressed. Before I could chivvy her along, the rest of the family arrived. My sister's Border terrier Nelson was always a popular visitor, and today proved no exception. While my sister entertained a number of questions from the residents, the rest of us looked on, except for Mum who was asking Nan why she wasn't ready.

Shortly, Mrs Caunter, the Templars manager entered the room and announced herself to the family. Nan rolled her eyes and made her usual face of contempt towards Mrs Caunter. She didn't like the woman, but had the good sense not to vent her opinions out loud, as she habitually did with her fellow residents. Vocabulary that Nan had used to describe Mrs Caunter in the past included smarmy, smug, self-important and shallow, which eventually earned her the nickname Mrs Bighead.

Having exchanged pleasantries with the family, Mrs Caunter bent down to stroke Nelson.

"Bite her!"

Although not as loud as usual, Nan's words were audible enough to draw a reproachful look from Mum. Fortunately, Mrs Caunter appeared not to have heard or chose not to react. Once Mrs Caunter had left the room, Mum tackled Nan about her behaviour.

"She wouldn't have heard me," Nan laughed quite indignantly.

"People do hear what you say. You forget you can't hear well, so you shout sometimes without even realising it," Mum remonstrated. The rest of us were largely unsupportive, and just grinned and chuckled, which doubtless encouraged Nan to rebel further.

Eventually, after some to and froing from Nan's room, we were ready to embark on our journey. Despite the relative warmth of the day, an extra jumper and blanket were packed into a holdall for the trip. Nan had a habit of complaining about the cold, even when the temperature was quite the opposite.

This was probably the very first occasion that I had had Nan to myself for any length of time; our family always seemed to visit together. As children and teenagers, we are often too concerned with our own lives to appreciate that older family members might have led a very interesting and different life. It is only when we grow older and more appreciative of the world around us, that we do become more curious.

The very first question I wanted to ask Nan was along the lines of 'What did you do in the war?' or 'What was it like during the war?' I resisted leaping straight in, since I knew from conversations with my other relatives that many old people who lived through those dark days preferred not to revisit their experiences, and Nan was no exception. Instead, I decided to focus on her childhood and leave the war until another occasion.

1918-1932

Mabel Jean Hill (née Ellis) was born during the final six months of World War I on 10th May 1918. She was an unplanned addition to her family, and the youngest of five children. Her eldest brother had already left home by the time she was born to her then 41-year-old mother. By the time she was eight years old, only her sister Di, who was six years older, remained at the family home.

At the time of her birth, the small Hertfordshire market town of Baldock consisted of fewer than ten streets; today it is an ever-expanding town of nearly 15000 residents. Mabel's family, like many in the town, lived in a traditional two-up, two-down terrace house with an outside toilet. Mabel, though often a serious and solemn child especially when it came to having her photo taken, was a very obedient young girl who was always eager to please. As an eight-year-old she helped her mother around the house; cleaning, washing and preparing meals.

Her family, although working-class, ate well and had a remarkably well-balanced diet for those times. This was largely as a result of her father's allotment which supplemented the general stodge of bread and potatoes, commonplace at this time, with an array of freshly grown vegetables, peas and runner beans, his youngest daughter's favourites. Mabel ate well and enjoyed the odd treat such as her beloved condensed milk on toast, an indulgence she would continue to have for the rest of her life, and one that she later introduced to her own daughters.

Mabel's father George, like most of the men in Baldock, worked in a brewery. Simpson's brewery was the largest in the town and employed over 70 people. Mabel wasn't sure exactly what her father did there, but knew it was something to do with the barrels. Many of the thirty or so pubs in Baldock at that time served Simpson's fine ales; today no breweries remain open and just 10 pubs survive. The slogan 'fine ales' puzzled Mabel as she couldn't understand why it was called 'fine'. She thought the taste of the foul brown liquid her father so proudly allowed her to try once was quite disgusting! Simpson's 'foul ales' would have been much more appropriate in her opinion.

Mabel's mother, Mary, worked on the spinning floor of the Full-Fashioned Hosiery Company off Mansfield Road. Later to be renamed Kayser Bondor, Mabel too would work at FFHC later in her life. Both her parents were out of the house for long periods, especially her father, who after a long day's toil at the brewery, would disappear after the evening meal either to the allotment in spring and summer, or to the Orange Tree public house every Friday and Saturday on receiving his weekly pay packet.

Mabel and her sister Di would always be the first one's home after a day at school, and between them would set about several jobs around the house. Mabel's tasks typically included scrubbing the front door step, sweeping the floors, and preparing vegetables for the evening meal harvested by her father the previous evening. Di being older and stronger would sometimes operate the mangle, as Mabel was too small to use it successfully.

Although Mabel and Di were extremely different in temperament, they got on very well. At times they were constantly arguing, especially if they had been in each other's company too long, but they shared a deep and loving friendship which bonded them together. Being six years older than Mabel, and with their parents working long hours, Di took it upon herself to look out for her younger sister, both at home and school. Consequently, the girls spent a lot of time together. One of their favourite pastimes was playing cards. Di had been taught by their maternal grandmother who had died two years previously. Mabel could just about remember visiting her along with her older two sisters. Occasionally they would play for small sums of money, but for the most part it was for matchsticks.

Once Di turned 16, she and Mabel slowly began to drift apart. Di had given up a part-time job in the laundry at Baldock convent and was now working full-time. She was also of the age at which a husband could be found. Having once been a regular visitor to the cinema with Mabel, it was now a long line of male suitors who would accompany her.

It wasn't long before one of these relationships developed into something more serious. Eddie Waterhouse was just 18 years old, in the army, and billeted nearby. A whirlwind romance ended in an engagement for 17-year-old Di and marriage a year later. While Mabel was delighted at the thought of being a bridesmaid, she also faced the prospect of losing a sister and a friend. Di had decided to move with her new husband to Gloucester where his family lived. It was a time of great happiness for the Ellis family, but also one tinged with sadness at Di's departure.

Mabel's first experience of work came at the age of 12 when she was employed as a part-time cleaner at Grove House School in Whitehorse Street. Di's part-time job in the laundry at Baldock convent was still available, but Mabel was put off for two reasons. The convent was on the outskirts of the town down a long and, in winter, dark track known locally as the Cinder Path. Mabel wasn't especially afraid of the dark but she preferred not to, all the same. Di also told her that the French nuns were very strict and made her work extremely hard.

Each day after finishing her lessons at Pond Lane School, Mabel would walk the five minutes it took her to reach her place of employment. She liked her job very much. Grove House was a small private school for girls which catered for both day and residential students.

She would start upstairs by cleaning the girls' bedrooms. The contrast to her own sparse bedroom was striking, but Mabel was not the type of girl to get jealous. Instead, she marvelled at their belongings, hoping one day she would be able to buy such things. There was one bedroom in particular that she liked and admired. Each day as she cleaned it, she would eye the array of intriguing objects with growing curiosity, so wanting to pick them up but frightened that she would be caught. Encased in an expensive looking silver frame, a photograph of two young girls and, presumably, their parents, all with broad smiles, particularly appealed to her.

Next to the photograph was a beautifully crafted set of hairbrushes with patterned cream and brown ceramic backings. Trailing from them were strands of mousey brown hair that weaved in and out of the bristles. Beyond these were a number of bottles, each containing different coloured liquids. Again, the temptation to touch them, unscrew the lids and smell the unusual potions was powerful, but one that Mabel resisted.

After completing the bedrooms, she would make her way downstairs just in time for class dismissal, ready for her to sweep, clean and dust the classrooms. She didn't like her own school; the lessons were boring, and Mabel recoiled further at the idea of attending a school where they finished even later. She was under strict instructions to avoid any conversation or contact with the girls.

This remained the case until one day a voice called out from behind her as she left the school and started to walk home. Mabel froze, somewhat startled, and then slowly began to turn around, worried that she had done something wrong when performing her cleaning job.

"Is it Mabel? I heard Mrs Datchworth call you by that name?" A smartly dressed girl with two mousey pigtails stood in front of her. She was about the same age as Mabel, but it was the strange accent that puzzled her.

Mabel hesitated and stumbled to find a reply, aware that she didn't want to break the headmistress's rules by talking to one of the students, and thus end up losing her job. "… Er…yes," she stammered.

"Hello, I'm Brigitte," replied the young girl, holding out her right hand.

Reluctantly Mabel took hold of the proffered hand and shook it, at the same time casting a nervous glance over the girl's shoulder to make sure nobody from the school was watching.

"Can I walk with you?" Brigitte asked.

Mabel hesitated once more, "I suppose so," and then remembering her manners continued, "yes, that would be very nice."

Mabel and her new friend started to walk along Whitehorse Street past the Victoria public house to the junction with Church Street.

"So, you clean our rooms and school Mabel?"

"Yes, I do."

"Is it very hard work?"

"No, not really, you all keep your rooms so tidy."

"Do you go to school Mabel?"

"Yes, I go to Pond Lane School."

"Is that in Baldock?"

Mabel replied that it was, and Brigitte proceeded to ask her many more questions about her school and life in Baldock. By this time, they had almost reached Mabel's house, when Brigitte paused and inquired, "Don't you want to ask me any questions?"

Mabel looked Brigitte up and down, before sheepishly replying, "I'm not allowed to."

"I know," a beaming Brigitte replied, "it's rather silly, isn't it?"

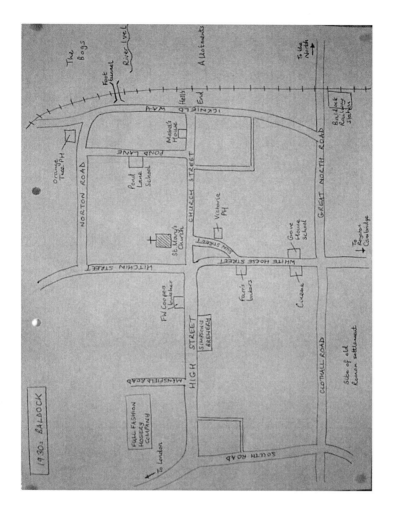

"Yes, I suppose it is," replied Mabel. "This is where I live so I had better go now. I have jobs to do for my mother."

"Can we chat again soon?"

"Yes, that would be nice. Thank you."

"Bye."

Mabel walked up the step to her house, opened the front door, and gave Brigitte a small wave before closing the door.

The next day, after school, Mabel walked along her usual route to Grove House. After collecting her cleaning materials, she trudged up the stairs to clean the first bedroom. On entering it she was greeted by a smiling Brigitte who sat on her bed dressed in a pair of patterned flannelette pyjamas.

"Hello Mabel." On seeing the look of worry spread across Mabel's face, Brigitte quickly added, "It's all right, I'm not very well," and then gave Mabel an exaggerated wink. "I've cleaned my room, so you won't have too today. I'd like to carry on with our chat from yesterday."

"Do your teachers know you are here?" asked Mabel, a little concerned that she was about to be caught and reprimanded for talking to Brigitte.

"No, they think I'm in the rest room, so you won't get into trouble. Get one of your dusters out and you can pretend to be dusting if anyone comes in."

Mabel was quite shocked by this suggestion. She'd had a strict upbringing and always obeyed rules. She knew that she could expect to be disciplined harshly if she stepped out of line.

Brigitte Duval was the same age as Mabel and, along with her father, had temporarily left their French homeland in order for Mr Duval to set up a UK branch of the fixings and fasteners factory he had founded. Since her mother and older sister had both died in a tragic train crash, her father had no choice but to bring Brigitte to England. Mr Duval rented a room at one of Baldock's old coaching inns, and Brigitte became a boarder at Grove House. She was not, however, enjoying her new life.

"I'm so bored Mabel. Class is so long and tedious, and then I'm stuck in my room for ages. Papa works such long hours that I only get to see him on weekends."

"I don't like school either."

"Take me on a tour of Baldock, Mabel."

"I can't now, I've got my cleaning job."

"Not now!" Brigitte reassured her, "when you are free and I'm better!"

"I'm not sure when that would be. I have lots of jobs to do at home."

"Don't worry, we'll find a way."

Brigitte was determined to get her own way, and hatched a plan to help Mabel finish her chores at home more rapidly allowing the two of them to spend more time together.

So that the two girls could meet for as long as possible, Mabel started her cleaning chores the following morning so that there would be less to do after school, but also because she wanted to present her home in the best possible light to her new friend. She was aware that other people lived in far larger and grander houses, but she was content with her lot and would not be embarrassed. Brigitte's family were obviously wealthier than her own, but the French girl was very nice and didn't seem to care about material items. On leaving Grove House later that day, Mabel found Brigitte a short way along Whitehorse Street peering through a window of the Victoria public house.

"An English bar, but so much grander than the ones we have back at home. I love the oak panel work, and so many glasses. Do you go in there Mabel?"

Mabel explained that she was too young, but that she had been in a pub garden. Brigitte appeared confused with this information, but she didn't question Mabel any further.

"Ah, la boulangerie," Brigitte exclaimed.

"The what…?" Mabel enquired.

"La boulangerie, the bakers," Brigitte raised one of her hands towards the shop window of Farr's bakers.

"La bowl orangey?" Mabel tried to repeat what Brigitte had just said.

"La boulangerie," Brigitte corrected, and helped Mabel practise the correct pronunciation until she could produce a half-decent version.

"Et l'épicerie, the grocers." Mabel again repeated the French name for the shop. This continued for almost every shop they walked past. Mabel was fascinated to be learning a new language, but at the same time not forgetting that she had chores to complete at home.

The long line of pig carcasses that hung outside F.W. Cooper's butchers encouraged fits of laughter as she repeated 'cochon' time and time again.

When they did eventually reach Mabel's house, it was a good job that she did have a helper because there was very little time left before her parents would arrive home. If Brigitte was shocked by the compactness and spartan nature of Mabel's home, she didn't show it, and further extended the hand of friendship by inviting her to the Baldock Picture House at the weekend. Mabel rarely went to the cinema these days. The last time she'd been was with her sister Di before she got married, so she was delighted to be asked.

Saturday afternoons were the only times in the week which Mabel always had to herself, free from helping in and around the home. The Saturday afternoon matinee consisted of several small presentations and one longer feature. Brigitte insisted on paying for both tickets costing four-pence and also bought a bar of KitKat and tube of Rolos for three-pence. Going to the pictures was one of Mabel's favourite pastimes, and she particularly liked the children's adventure films. She soon discovered these were Brigitte's favourites too. The two girls, determined to have their own adventure, quickly formulated plans on how to put this into action. Eventually, they decided to build their own camp or hide, and after drawing out countless designs, fixed upon one that they would build. With the school holidays looming, both girls would have extra time to fulfil their plans.

A few days later, Mabel introduced Brigitte to their own special place that would bond their friendship forever. This time they walked the whole length of Church Street and onto Icknield Way, often nicknamed Hell's End because of the absolute poverty and destitution of its inhabitants. Mabel could see that Brigitte was a bit shocked, but she quickly regained her composure as they walked among the ramshackle housing. Beyond the towering gas station at the end of the houses stood the tracks of the Great Northern Railway which carried the impressive beasts of steam trains belching out columns of smoke as they made their way back-and-forth to London King's Cross. Fortunately, the tracks were perched high up on an embankment thereby sparing the unfortunate residents of this poor quarter of Baldock the worst of the pollution.

Cut deep into the foot of the embankment was a foot tunnel, unlit and with water dripping down from the arched brick roof. An atmosphere of dampness and claustrophobia prevailed. This was the gateway to the land of adventure that Brigitte so badly craved. The 'Bogs', so called because the town's sewers were located here, were in fact the source of the river Ivel with marshes on either side of the small floodplain. Despite this the waters for the most part were clear and an abundance of water-cress swamped the chalk river bed. Further out from the river's right bank were the allotments that Mabel's father tended. The left bank was much more secluded and interesting with a larger stretch of marshland, a wooded area and beyond that a rubbish tip which served the town.

Exploring the Bogs were some of the most carefree days Mabel and Brigitte would spend in their entire lives. Hunting for birds' nests, catching newts and frogs, and constructing a rope swing were just some of the activities they enjoyed. Armed with the drawing of their ideal camp, Brigitte appreciated the potential of the area.

"Perfect!" Brigitte exclaimed as an enormous grin spread across her face. "Now to look for somewhere to build a camp."

Weaving a path carefully through the marshes, Mabel took care not to let Brigitte get her nice shoes wet and dirty. She also recalled the many adventures she had also enjoyed with her sister in summers past. The adjacent overgrown woodland appeared to be the most likely site for building a camp, and Brigitte soon discovered the perfect location. Down a small embankment, and next to the river, was a well-hidden concave indentation in the bank with small trees hiding the entrance. The next thing the two girls had to do was to construct a waterproof outer shell for their new hide.

Fortunately, the nearby rubbish tip provided a wealth of material, such as corrugated iron and offcuts of wood. Working tirelessly over the school holidays a surprisingly comfortable residence was constructed by the girls. Some camouflage was added and rendered the hide virtually invisible to the outside world. Brigitte had bought some personal effects from her room to add to the items they had rescued from the dump.

Over time, the friends would add more ornaments and other effects. Many long and deep discussions took place about their lives, boys and what they hoped the future held. Brigitte continued to teach Mabel French.

One afternoon, while sitting in their hideaway, Brigitte shocked Mabel with an idea. Even though Mabel had become more confident as a result of her friendship with Brigitte she was still reluctant to engage in risk-taking, or indeed anything which broke the rules.

"Why don't we sleep here one night?"

"My parents wouldn't allow me," replied Mabel quietly.

"No! We don't ask, we sneak out one night without anyone knowing. Think about what an adventure it would be."

Mabel appeared dumbstruck and didn't volunteer a reply.

"Please say yes. We'll come up with a perfect plan. I promise you that you won't get caught."

Reluctantly, and after much pleading by Brigitte, Mabel agreed. They would put their plan into action the following Friday. Brigitte knew that there were fewer overnight staff at the school during the weekend, and Mabel's father always slept well after spending the evening supping ale at the Orange Tree. Brigitte intended to creep out of the school just after midnight and wait for Mabel to join her at the back entrance to the churchyard, just a few yards from Mabel's house.

On the day before their midnight adventure, at the request of Brigitte, Mabel carried out a dummy run. Lying in bed, she felt a nervous excitement as the interminable gaps between the church bells chiming every quarter of an hour grew. On one hand it was pointless trying to sleep because she was just too much on edge to do so; alternatively, she didn't want to risk nodding off and messing up the dummy run.

Mabel heard her parents mount the creaky, uncarpeted stairs at a little after 10pm. Both would have had long tiring days at work, and faced getting up early the next morning, so she knew they would be asleep very quickly. The next hour and a half dragged even more slowly than Mabel could have imagined. Once she thought her parents must be asleep, she quietly pushed her bed covers off, tiptoed across the room and drew back the curtains.

The moonlight streamed into her room casting a spidery shadow on the far wall as the trees in the adjacent churchyard distorted the moon's silver rays. Mabel looked down into the small rectangular backyard, eyeing the route she had worked out earlier.

After taking a few deep breaths to calm her nerves, Mabel opened one of the windows and moved a wooden chair next to it. Clambering onto the window sill, she nimbly lowered herself onto the coalhouse roof as gently as she could, since the corrugated iron roof was unforgiving, should any heavy object land on it unexpectedly. Having made her way down to the roof's edge, Mabel lowered herself to the ground using the guttering and adjacent brick wall. She then quietly made her way along the alley at the side of the house and paused at the entrance to the street.

Mabel stood in complete darkness, the still eeriness of the night sending a shiver down her spine. Neither a soul nor sound could be seen or heard, only the moonlight illuminating the opposite side of the street gave any shape or form to the surroundings. The emptiness of the street gave her some reassurance that they would be able to carry out their plan the following evening. Mabel then withdrew from the street and retraced her path until she was safely back in her bed and quickly fast asleep.

Next day proved to be a difficult one for Mabel. She was reprimanded on more than one occasion by her teacher for not paying attention in class. Later, at Grove House, she managed a few brief words with Brigitte as planned, to inform her how the dummy run had gone and to confirm that tonight would go ahead.

That night, Mabel again waited patiently until she was sure her parents were asleep. Once the church bells chimed at half past eleven, she began to carry out the procedure she had practised the night before. Drawing back the curtains, she was shocked that the moon was nowhere to be seen; in fact, she saw nothing but darkness. After fumbling around to find her coat, she felt for the window catch and slowly opened it.

With her heartbeat now far above its usual rate, Mabel began to fear what the night might hold for her. What had seemed so easy the night before had now become a very tricky and difficult task. Despite this, she successfully eased herself down onto the corrugated roof of the coalhouse without making a noise. The next manoeuvre would be the trickiest, lowering herself down from the shed roof to ground level, and unfortunately for Mabel it proved to be so. Crash! She had landed on the upturned bath tub, causing it to topple over and make several loud bangs as it hit the concrete floor and continued to rock from side to side.

Shocked and momentarily stunned by what had happened, Mabel looked up at her open window, half-expecting to see her father. Without a second thought, she quickly shinned up the guttering and tiptoed as quickly as she could across the coalhouse roof to the open window. Once she had climbed back in, the bedroom door opened and her father stood there.

"What are you doing Mabe?" he asked. Only her father used this shortened form of her name.

Mabel, still standing by the open window, replied slightly nervously, "I heard a noise and went to see what it was?"

"Why have you got your coat on?"

"I thought I might go down and have a look."

"No, get back into bed, I will go down and check."

Mabel did as she was told and clambered back into bed. She knew she was already several minutes late for the rendezvous with Brigitte, and just hoped that her friend wouldn't make her way to the house and bump into father whom she could hear out in the backyard setting the bath tub back into an upturned position. It appeared to be fine, because in a few minutes she heard her father's footsteps trundling up the wooden staircase, and the bedroom door close behind him.

Next day was a Saturday, and Brigitte was due to meet her own father, Mr Duval, so Mabel probably wouldn't see her friend until Monday, which was frustrating since she so wanted to explain what had happened. She felt her unpreparedness and failure to plan for the unexpected had let Brigitte down, and she badly wanted to apologise.

Having moped around for most of the weekend, Mabel felt in a much better mood on Monday morning. Even her mother remarked on this, since Mabel was normally always in a bad mood every Monday and never one to look forward to school. Once lessons had finished for the day, Mabel hurried down to Grove House, arriving slightly earlier than usual.

Brigitte's bedroom was always the first to be cleaned, but to her horror the room was completely bare. No trace of Brigitte existed. Mabel stood stunned for a moment. Where was her friend? Most people would have moved on and cleaned the next room, but Mabel was always very thorough and dedicated, which meant that she proceeded to clean the room. Brigitte obviously had anticipated this, since she had concealed between the bed linen and the wall her French-English dictionary. Mabel pulled the book out from its hiding-place and opened it. Inside the front cover, a scribbled note read 'M, I've had to go away. All my love B x.' How clever of Brigitte to use letters instead of full names, since had one of the staff found the note, Mabel would not get into trouble.

Tears welled up in Mabel's eyes; this was a cruel shock. She really wanted to take off and find somewhere quiet to think about all that had happened. Instead, she knew that she had to finish her cleaning for the day. Mabel tried hard to concentrate. At least she had Brigitte's dictionary, and she was determined to teach herself more French.

One day she would meet Brigitte again. She was sure of that.

*

The clear skies present on leaving Baldock accompanied us on the whole of our journey, which pleased Nan since she had always been something of a sun worshipper. Even as recently as her late eighties she had enjoyed holidaying on the Spanish Costas. The traffic was a little heavy once we reached the outskirts of Gloucester. As we queued, an adjacent car's loud music blared out from an open window.

"Excellent, a mobile disco," Nan commented in her most sarcastic voice, "and why is it that drivers who insist on sharing their music always have such poor taste?"

I laughed. As usual Nan was spot-on in her appraisal; it did always seem to be naff, thudding disco sound which emanated from these vehicles.

On our arrival, driving into the church hall car park, Nan instructed me to park as close as I could to the entrance to the garden where, as a result of the exceptionally mild weather, a good number of Di's family and friends had gathered. I knew that Nan was extremely proud of her good health and would want to walk unaided to join the party. At Mum's insistence, and much to Nan's chagrin, the wheelchair had been secreted in the car boot. I knew that it wouldn't be making an appearance. I also knew it would be pointless to ask Nan if she needed any assistance to make her way to the gathering, but I did so anyway, only to receive a sharp and decisive brush-off. I walked as close as I could get away with, without giving to those assembled the impression I was supporting her.

The conversation stopped and the guests turned around as we entered. This was, I suppose, a significant piece of Ellis family history. The first ever centurion of the family, joined by what would probably be the second centenarian in a few years' time, and the only other member of her generation still alive. A chair, much to my relief, was quickly vacated so that Nan could sit next to her sister. Di rose up out of her chair, extremely sprightly for a woman of her years. Both women embraced, paused and communicated a few private inaudible words, before hugging again. I suspected they would have liked to have spoken in private, but this was never going to happen. Di was swiftly presented with a birthday cake, and a rendition of 'Happy Birthday' commenced.

Following what seemed like an endless photo session, both with mobiles and conventional cameras, the two sisters entertained a number of questions. Most concerned their longevity, though neither seemed to have any idea for what reason they numbered nearly 200 years between them. Both had smoked until their sixties, sprinkled copious amounts of salt on their food, and one had been teetotal virtually all their life while the other had drank alcohol virtually every day.

While Di and Nan were enjoying the attention thrust upon them, I happily withdrew to be with the rest of my close family, asking Mum to point out certain relatives I had not seen for many years. Di had already outlived two of her six children, and her husband Eddie who had been dead for nearly thirty years. Of her remaining children, who lined up proudly by her side as the photos continued, it was clear one of her sons didn't particularly resemble any of his siblings. According to Mum it was always rumoured that Di had several affairs and John was the result of one of them.

By 4 pm it was time to make the two-hour return trip. Nan had clearly enjoyed herself and spoke about making a return journey in the near future. In the car I had hoped to pursue our earlier conversation, but it soon became clear that Nan had worn herself out, so much so that she slept the entire way home.

Chapter 2

The next time I visited Nan was a full week later. I was eager for her to continue her life story, but appreciated that she needed to fully recuperate from the exertion of last week's journey and party. The recent upturn in the weather had persisted as temperatures topped 20°C for the first time that year. I realised that this would be a good opportunity to take Nan out for a walk and continue our conversation from the previous week. I decided to visit just after lunch, which meant that the temperature would hold up for another hour or so. It would also be highly unlikely that Nan would have any other visitors. If she did, I knew it would be improbable that she would speak about her earlier life as she had done on our journey to Gloucester.

Lunch had just finished when I arrived, the distinctive smell of fish and chips pervading every corner and niche of Templars. Nan was one of the first to have made her way to the residents' lounge, where she sat in her usual spot, sunning herself by the south-facing windows, with a smug look on her face.

"What have you done?" I asked, trying to keep a smirk off my face.

"Just keeping the old hag on her toes."

The 'old hag' was one of the many names Nan reserved for Mrs Caunter.

"So, what have you done?" I tried again, this time raising my eyebrows and trying to look stern.

"Nothing much," Nan's grin grew wider as she began to chuckle, "Look at the chair to my left."

There was a large wet patch on the chair. I raised my eyebrows again.

"Did you do that?"

Nan laughed, "It's not what you think."

"What is it then?"

As more residents trickled back into the lounge following lunch, Nan appeared to appreciate for once that it would be a good idea to lower her voice.

"It's only water, but the old hag will think one of the gangs has peed themselves!"

"Why would you want to do that?"

"It will be funny seeing her rushing around, interfering and making a fool of herself. All for some spilt water."

"Have you done this before then?"

Nan hesitated before answering, "Maybe once or twice."

"Right, let's take you out for a walk before you cause any more trouble."

My second 'travel with my Nan' was a much shorter one, to Baldock's Kayser Bondor memorial garden, just a ten-minute walk from Templars. Kayser Bondor was the name of a clothing factory originally called the Full Fashion Hosiery Company. Opened in 1926, it became Kayser Bondor just after the end of World War Two, and eventually closed in 1982. Like many textile companies in the United Kingdom, it ceased trading due to cheaper imports from abroad.

In inter-war years Baldock, those who didn't work in one of the breweries, almost certainly worked at the FFHC. During its heyday, in very different social times, the company provided no less than two tennis courts, an outdoor swimming pool, gardens and a ballroom for its employees. As a young boy I could remember visiting the pool with its unheated and seemingly freezing cold water. Sadly, the pool has since been filled in and remains hidden beneath a car park for the Tesco Extra which now occupies the site of the old factory.

I decided that taking Nan to the memorial garden would be the next logical step in my quest to find out what she did during the war. The memorial garden, tucked away in a quiet corner of the vast car park, and fortunately screened by trees, commemorated FFHC employees who had fought and lost their lives during both World Wars. I knew that Nan's first full-time job after leaving Grove House had been at the FFHC just before the outbreak of World War Two, so it would be a good place to start. My plan was to ask her about her work here and gently nudge her into the war period.

1932-9

On leaving school at the age of 14, Mabel had increased her hours at Grove House where she continued to work until she turned 16. Thereafter she joined the workforce of the FFHC in 1934. Life for Mabel was pretty routine at this time. The extra wages were very welcome in the Ellis household, and for the first time since leaving school Mabel made new friends at the factory and went on the occasional date.

During 1938 as events moved rapidly across mainland Europe, they also changed for Mabel on the home front. Hitler's invasion of Czechoslovakia meant that the UK had to start preparing for the worst. Mabel was no longer making stockings, bras and knickers, but instead parachutes. Furthermore, part of the factory had been taken over and converted to a munitions workshop. This resulted in several more men on site, and it was one of these newcomers who caught her eye.

Herbert Reginald Hill, or HRH as he was nicknamed, had a cheeky smile which Mabel found hard to resist. However, it wasn't HRH that Mabel went out with initially. HRH's best mate, Bill Nicholson, also a Baldock boy, plucked up the courage to ask Mabel (and her best friend Gracie), on a date. As a foursome, they watched the latest release at the cinema before enjoying a fish and chip supper at Ma Blackwell's, the town's original fish and chip shop.

Next day the girls compared notes, and it soon became very apparent that they were dating the wrong ones, so next time Gracie went with Bill, and HRH with Mabel. The quartet began courting in 1938 and both couples married, just a few weeks apart, less than a year later in April 1939. The wedding was a joyous occasion with all four of Mabel's older siblings and their spouses in attendance. She was especially pleased that Di and Eddie had made the journey down from Gloucester.

Like most of the rest of the country, there was a shortage of housing so the newly married couple stayed in the Ellis household. Although Mabel's parents had since moved into a brand new three-bed council house on Norton Road, with two decent-sized double bedrooms and an inside toilet, the newlyweds would inevitably lack some privacy. She loved her parents dearly but so wanted a place of her own. In the town there were just a dozen or so council houses at this time, and private renting was increasingly hard to come by.

Mabel knew that an extra income would increase their chances of getting their first marital home, and decided to utilise her skills and experience from Grove House to secure some extra hours at FFHC by taking on evening cleaning duties. She realised that it would be hard work, and leave her exhausted, but it wouldn't be forever. Mabel began her cleaning job in late summer, just weeks before the outbreak of war. She had always been a worrier, and the prospect of war scared her.

Parachute production was in full flow now, and turned out to be much harder work than making stockings. The material was much coarser and harder to work with, and of course quality control demanded the very highest standards. Once the dome canopy had been cut out the suspension lines needed to be fitted along with the ripcord which required metal connectors to hold the steel cable in place. Mabel found the work tough on her hands, which quickly lost their silky smoothness of her youth.

The early days of the war brought a mixture of fear and excitement for Mabel. Herbie had enlisted in the army and was away for months on end, not that she had much chance to miss him; her long days were often followed by disturbed, sleepless nights courtesy of the Luftwaffe.

One evening after completing her shift making parachutes, Mabel felt particularly tired as she walked to collect her cleaning materials from the storeroom where they were kept. Having been on her feet all day, Mabel uncharacteristically decided to have a five-minute breather before she started the job. Sitting down among the clothes, rags and buckets, she used one of the brooms to reach over and push the door shut. She didn't want to be caught skiving, but she felt she really needed to rest her weary limbs for five minutes or so. Mabel's tiredness caught up with her though, and she slid into deep sleep.

On waking, Mabel was understandably confused; on her own and confined in a pitch-black cupboard on a pile of rags she initially began to panic before realising where she was. Once the thudding of her heart had abated, she got to her feet and quietly opened the cupboard door. Darkness met her wary eyes, and instantly she was reminded of the occasion when she was 12 years old and, on her way, to meet her childhood French friend Brigitte Duval.

Slowly the faint shafts of moonlight helped Mabel make out the silhouettes of the tall thin factory windows, and gradually the layout of the work benches and machinery. It then occurred to her that she hadn't even started her cleaning duties. Edging over to the windows Mabel angled her wristwatch skywards to read its hands. Half past eight, she had slept for over two hours. Horrified, she tried to think clearly as to what she should do. Her hours were from six to eight o'clock, so she wouldn't be missed much back at home just yet, but that would soon change if she didn't start to walk home immediately.

The factory blackouts were up, but she knew her family would worry, so she had no option but to leave the factory and walk home. She decided she would have to get in first tomorrow morning and attempt some quick tidying-up, and just hope her inadequacy wouldn't be noticed. Mabel dreaded the shame it would bring upon her family if she were to be sacked.

Aware that the night watchman may be on site somewhere, Mabel tiptoed to the cloakroom to retrieve her coat. While fastening the buttons, she glanced through one of the small cloakroom windows which overlooked the packing department. A small silvery object bobbing around caught her eye. Mabel stood very still. The packing room was dark except for the moonlight from two high windows which cast a shadow across the room. Mabel strained her eyes to adjust them and work out what the object was. It continued to move up and down, and occasionally in a forward motion.

After a while she became aware of a shadowy figure beside it. With her heartbeat accelerating and sweat beginning to accumulate on the palms of her hands, Mabel edged closer to the window. Fortunately, the cloakroom was in almost complete darkness so she was confident of remaining undetected.

She continued to stare at the figure as more things in the room became clear to her. The mystery person appeared to be rummaging around in some of the packed parachutes. The dusty cloakroom window wasn't giving her the best view, but she questioned whether she could actually risk creeping into the packaging room and investigating further. Perhaps she should find an alternative plan.

As quickly as she could, without making a noise or colliding with any work surfaces or other sizable and potentially noise-producing obstacles, Mabel stealthily tiptoed to the packing room. She found the door closed; there was no possibility that she would be able to open the door without being heard or seen by the shadowy figure inside.

It was then that Mabel, who amazed herself with her quick thinking, decided to enter the packing room via the delivery hatch from the main production floor. Increasingly aware that the intruder could leave at any time, she rushed to the delivery hatch; her experience of cleaning the factory helped her negotiate a route without any noisy accidents. Mabel slowly levered herself up onto the hatch so that she could see into the packing room. The shadowy figure stood with its back to Mabel, slightly hunched over some parachutes. She continued to observe the figure, which appeared to be opening one of the parachute parcels and then cutting the suspension lines with scissors before repacking them. The scissors, then, were the shiny object that she had seen through the cloakroom window.

The big question was what Mabel should do next. The advantage of approaching the figure from the delivery hatch was that he or she had their back to her but, if Mabel made any noise, then she had at least 20 feet and a maze of benches to negotiate, giving her prey quite a head start. She could search for the night watchman to assist her, but that would take a good ten minutes to run to the entry gate and back, during which time the intruder might escape. Old Eddie Hutchinson, the long-serving night-watchman, was not far from retirement and not the most mobile on his feet, so Mabel wasn't convinced that would be the best solution anyway.

Very quickly the situation changed as the intruder began replacing the parachute parcels back on the shelves where they sat ready for despatch. Sensing he or she would be leaving soon, and desperate to prevent this, Mabel quickly lowered herself down from the delivery hatch and into the packing room. Picking up one of the unpacked parachutes, probably not the best improvised weapon she could find, Mabel tiptoed towards the figure as close as she could sensibly risk, rushed forward and threw the open parachute onto the intruder who began to turn around. Momentarily shocked that the figure was female, Mabel grabbed the intruder who was grappling with the opened parachute and struggling to shed it. The slightly-built figure began to yell out in anger as Mabel gripped the flailing arms as tightly as she could.

Surprised that the intruder was in fact a young girl, near to her own age, Mabel grew in confidence, and used her leg to trip the figure up and send it tumbling onto the stone floor. The girl continued to struggle but, with the weight of Mabel's body on top of her, she lacked the strength to make any headway.

What to do next would test Mabel's resolve and determination even more than apprehending the interloper. She needed to decide how to continue to hold the girl, and at the same time get some assistance. Mabel considered calling out for help, but the factory was a large site and Eddie was probably sitting in his office with his feet up. She really didn't want to show her captive that she wasn't in full control of the situation, so another alternative had to be found.

Mabel scanned the packing room, desperately looking for a solution, when her eyes fell upon a roll of packing string. Joy quickly turned to disappointment when she realised that it was beyond her reach. Still sitting on her quarry, she grabbed one of the parachutes off the adjacent bench and pulled it out. Using the scissors, she managed to cut some of the suspension lines free from the canopy. Having cut four fairly long lengths of cord, Mabel decided to tie the girl's legs together first, since these were exposed beneath the parachute canopy, so this seemed to be the easiest thing to do.

45

The girl, who had been settled for five minutes, doubtless preserving her energy, made a determined effort to break free as Mabel turned her body to face the girl's feet and legs. However, she was ready for this tactic; years of play-fighting with her older sister Di ensured this. Before the girl was aware what was happening, Mabel had thrust a piece of cord under her writhing torso. She started to draw in the arms tightly to the body, and proceeded to tie several knots to keep the cord in place. The girl continued to struggle like snared fish flapping around as they are hauled from a river. After securing a further piece of cord around the girl's legs, Mabel sat up and leant back, resting her exhausted body against one of the benches, breathing heavily and feeling her heart thudding against her ribcage. Thinking it not wise to rest for long, she stood up, checked the blackouts were in place before turning the lights on. The girl who lay face down on the floor with both arms and legs tied up, turned her face towards Mabel. Probably the same age as Mabel, the young woman angrily shouted, "Let me go. You'll be sorry you did this."

Mabel recognised her captive from the canteen kitchen. She wasn't a Baldock girl and had started work at the FFHC only the previous week. Ignoring her threats, Mabel hurried across the packing room floor to the telephone and rang the night-watchman's office. After what seemed five very long rings Eddie answered the phone, (probably having a nap Mabel concluded). Once she had told Eddie what had happened, she sat down and waited for the police to arrive. Within two- or three-minutes Eddie had joined her, putting his arm around her to comfort her.

"You'll be quite a local heroine when this gets out Mabel, and so brave. I can see it now – 'photo and interview' in the local paper,"

Eddie gave Mabel a friendly pat on her back. She winced, not at Eddie's sympathetic touch, but the thought of being in the local paper. She would prefer to avoid the limelight, but on reflection it had been an exciting evening. Mabel felt proud that she had single-handedly stepped in and thwarted an act of sabotage.

A couple of hours later, Mabel was at last in her own bed, very much awake and finding it hard to relax sufficiently to slip into sleep. Earlier she had given a short statement to the police who had taken her home to face a further cross-examination from her parents! After their initial concern, there was no doubt that Mr and Mrs Ellis were extremely proud of their daughter.

A week later Mabel was summoned to see the manager of the FFHC. She had deliberately kept a low profile since apprehending the intruder. Not least because she didn't want any fuss made, but also, she was still conscious of the fact that she had neglected her cleaning duties that evening. It was with some trepidation that she approached the manager's office. This was only the second occasion she had visited Mr Morley's office; the first time on the day of her interview and appointment to the firm. Ernest Morley had been more than happy to hire Mabel. His family and Mabel's mother's family had known each other for several generations, and he trusted Mabel totally.

"Come in Mabel, and please sit down." Mr Morley's warm and generous smile immediately put Mabel at ease.

"Thank you, sir," Mabel replied as she positioned herself in a soft leather-cushioned chair.

"Mabel, I'd like to thank you very much for what you did last week. It was extremely brave of you. Let me tell you this – your action has saved many lives. Had those parachutes got on the backs of our young RAF men they would have stood no chance. The girl you caught was a saboteur, a member of a group who subscribe to Herr Hitler and his view that a German victory is inevitable. You, Mabel, are a huge credit to this firm and your country."

Mabel beamed with pleasure; never before had she been praised so richly. Morley leaned forward and spoke again, but this time in a low voice,

"What I'm about to tell you, Mabel, must not leave this room. Do you understand?"

Mabel wasn't really sure if she did, but nodded her head, assuming it would be some information about the young girl she had apprehended.

"Good. I belong to an organisation that is helping Britain fight this war. We give support to our armed forces and help them with information about the enemy. We are always on the look-out for patriotic and brave young people like you to help us out. I've known your family for a long time Mabel. I've watched you develop as a person, seen your confidence increase, and as I've already said what you did last week was exceptionally brave. Would you like to help us win the war Mabel?"

Mabel was unsure exactly what Mr Morley was asking but always eager to please, she replied in the affirmative. Morley smiled, before speaking again.

"The work we do is often quite dangerous, and in extreme cases you could be risking your life."

Morley paused to allow Mabel to take in this piece of information. Her confidence was probably at its highest point in the whole of her life; the capture of the saboteur had made her feel invincible, so he didn't want to take advantage of this.

"Would you be interested in joining our organisation, Mabel?"

Mabel thought of her HRH and all the other young men up and down the country who were risking their lives fighting the Germans. She was happy to join them.

"Yes, I would very much like to join. Thank you, sir."

"Well before you definitely say yes, let me first give you more details about what you would be involving yourself in. Then I'll give you a few days to think about it before making a final decision. I must add that you will be required to sign the Official Secrets Act and tell no one of your involvement, not even your parents."

Morley spent the next 20 minutes carefully explaining to Mabel what to expect. She would initially spend about four months training to become a special operative. The skills she would learn included how to shoot a firearm, how to trail subjects of interest without being detected, how to break into a building, and how to defend oneself against an attacker. The cover for this training that Mabel would tell her parents and friends was that she had been promoted within the FFHC and would join a team of buyers in London. Mabel would in fact be based in the countryside to the north-west of London, but she would communicate with her parents and husband via letter and be advised what to include about her new life in London. After her training she would then be assigned to a job. Some were in the UK, while others could be abroad. Some were short-term assignments, but most would last several months depending on the duration of the war.

On returning to her work area, Mabel had to strive extremely hard to suppress a huge smile that was trying to force its way onto her young face. She felt absolutely elated, and thoroughly excited at the prospect of her new role. As directed by Mr Morley, she told her work colleagues she had been with the manager to tie up a few loose ends over the intruder incident. She chose not to wait before informing Mr Morley of her decision, and instead did so the following day. Less than three days later she was waved off by her parents at Baldock station and on a train bound for King's Cross. She would in fact leave the train at Potters Bar where a car would drive her deep into the Buckinghamshire countryside.

*

I truly wanted to hear the next instalment of Nan's story, but the temperature had dropped rapidly during the last few minutes as the sinking sun fell behind the tops of the trees. I could also see that Nan was quite tired now, and in need of some refreshment. We were soon back at Templars where tea and biscuits were about to be served.

Unfortunately, as we entered the residents' lounge Mrs Caunter and one of her assistants were in deep conversation in front of the chair Nan had poured water onto. I tried to persuade Nan that a different chair in the room would suit her best, so that I could avoid having any discussion with Mrs Caunter about the chair. Nan was having none of it, and insisted on catching the sun's fading rays beside her usual window spot. Also, I have no doubt she wanted to know what exactly was going on!

"Just behave yourself," I warned her before wheeling her over to the chair.

Nan winked at me before allowing a smug grin to play around the corners of her lips. Predictably, Mrs Caunter asked to have a word with me.

"Do you know which chair Mabel was sitting in before you took her out?"

"That one," I replied pointing to the seat where she was now ensconced, and before I could stop myself, I found myself asking the one question I should have avoided.

"Why's that?"

"Oh, we think one of the residents has had a little accident," she replied, pointing to the chair. I couldn't bring myself to look directly at her for the fear of grinning or even starting to laugh. I just hoped that Nan wouldn't make some flippant comment. Fortunately, she didn't, and I left Mrs Caunter and her assistant to discuss their plan of action. Shaking my head, I addressed Nan as sternly as I could, without laughing, "No more, agreed?"

"Yes, OK then, as long as you don't blame me when it really happens."

Once the tea trolley had arrived, and Nan was content with a strong cup of tea and one of her favourite pink wafers, I bade her goodbye promising, I would visit soon and look forward to the next chapter of her life story.

Chapter 3

The unusually warm start to April had typically given way to a period of unsettled rainy weather. It was therefore impossible to take Nan out and enjoy the privacy afforded by a walk. This was most frustrating since the next part of her story was the instalment that I most wanted to hear.

The first decent day in terms of the weather, happened to be the 10th of May, the day of Nan's 95th birthday. Nan had chosen to start using her wheelchair, which surprised the rest of the family since she had always been so resistant. It seemed to please her three daughters who thought their mother was at last beginning to show some sense of responsibility regarding her health. I wasn't as convinced, and felt sure there was some ulterior motive. When the opportunity arose, I addressed her in her good ear, selecting a moment when everybody else appeared to be engaged in conversation.

"You can tell me next time what you are really up to!"

"What do you mean?" Nan's attempt at playing the innocent was somewhat lost when she allowed a large grin to cover her face.

"You know what I mean."

"Just getting around more easily."

"Yes, I'm sure you are." I replied sarcastically.

Our small family gathering to celebrate Nan's birthday was now assembled in one of the more sheltered gardens of Templars. The early afternoon sunshine had created a significant suntrap. One of my aunts started to unpack a couple of cooler bags of food and drink. The recurrent theme in the spread reflected Nan's favourite food; cheese sandwiches, cheese quiche, cheese and onion rolls, cheese and biscuits, and her favourite – freshly baked home-made cheese scones. If you weren't too fond of cheese there really wasn't much else for you except bread and assorted slices of meat. I suspected even the crisps were cheese and onion!

Much to everyone's amusement Nan made a big fuss when no salt cellar appeared on the table. She was famous for shaking copious amounts of the stuff onto whatever she happened to be eating. This was a habit she had acquired as a young girl, and she would not be dispensing with it anytime soon. This was despite the many warnings issued to her from all the family to cut down. She would always defend her salt intake, rightly claiming that it hadn't prevented her longevity. I could recall an incident about 15 years previously when we thought she had suffered a stroke, but it turned out to be a water infection.

After Nan had opened her presents and eaten some food, the topic of conversation inevitably turned to her advanced years, not only why she had lived to such an age, but also all the times and events she had lived through. Nan often became rather coy when asked about her early life, especially in front of an audience, and typically gave her stock answer 'I can't remember that far back'. None of the family believed her, as childhood memories tend to last a lifetime, but rarely would anyone challenge Nan to recall more. One of my uncles who had once asked Nan what she did during the war, decided to chance his arm once again. Having been met with her stock answer, one of my aunts tried to prompt her by asking where she worked during the war.

"At the Kayser Bondor."

Since the rest of the family were not born when the FFHC was in existence, Nan always referred to it as the Kayser Bondor which it became after the war.

"So, what did you do there during the war?" my aunt asked, sensing a breakthrough.

"Not a lot," Nan laughed.

"I bet you were on top-secret stuff Nan. That's why you can't say anything." I suggested.

"Dead right," Nan replied, "top-secret."

This response inevitably brought about a change in conversation, and was not mentioned again until it was time to leave.

"Thank you," whispered Nan as I bent down to kiss her goodbye. I was grateful for her appreciation, even though I knew full well that she was totally capable of abruptly halting any unwanted questions about her past.

A few days after Nan's birthday celebrations, I attended a talk given by the Baldock Museum and Local History Society on Roman Baldock. The town, once an important Roman settlement, was the meeting point of Roman roads from Colchester and Verulamium (now St Albans) which joined and eventually became Ermine Street further to the north. Although not directly relevant to this story, the meeting did provide me with two important finds to share with Nan.

Firstly, among the museum's significant treasure trove of old photographs was a whole album dedicated to the Kayser

Bondor. Crammed full of both pre- and post-war photographs I had briefly browsed through them after the talk had finished, in the hope of spotting Nan in one of them. Not wishing to prolong the departure of those who had given up their free time to very kindly host the evening, I decided I would bring Nan to the museum on another occasion.

The other 'find' was that Baldock has its own Facebook page for residents to upload old photographs of Baldock; 'The Old Baldock Pub Scrapbook'. As the warm and sunny weather had inevitably given way to windier and cloudier times, I decided to have a quick look at the site before visiting Nan next to see if I could find some old photographs of Baldock from her childhood. I knew she wouldn't venture out unless the sky was totally cloudless and the tree branches were perfectly still in the absence of any wind. I always wanted some purpose to my visits rather than pursuing the usual conversation along the lines of 'How are you today?' Nan never said anything, but I'm sure she must get fed up with the long line of bland questioning that seems to be commonplace in nursing and retirement homes.

I was surprised to discover that well over 500 photographs had been uploaded onto the site, but fortunately they had been categorised neatly into albums which made it a lot easier to track down relevant photographs. Once I had more time, I would have to go through the whole lot and share my findings with Nan. For the moment I settled on five photographs which I found and printed out: the Orange Tree public house, the original Baldock cinema, FW Coopers butcher, Church Street and Grove House School.

"You won't want to go out today, will you?" I enquired of Nan, having found her sitting in the communal lounge.

"No, it's too cold today," she replied.

I almost replied 'How would you know?' well aware that she hadn't been outside and had just observed the clouds from the window before coming to her judgement. It was in fact very humid and warm outside.

"Shall we go to your room then?"

"Yes."

Before we started looking at the photographs, I had one burning question that I needed to ask her.

"So why have you all of a sudden started to use your wheelchair?"

"It's quicker and easier to get around, and I need the rest." Nan replied, not entirely convincingly. It was very unusual of her to admit she needed help, which made me doubly suspicious.

"And what else?" I asked, keeping eye contact.

"OK then, I've been having some fun."

"What competing with some of the other residents in a wheelchair race?"

"No much more fun than that. I've been moving things around. Old big head doesn't know if she's coming or going."

"What have you been moving and why do you need the wheelchair?"

I began to wonder just how large and heavy some of these objects were.

"Just small things like items of clothing from one room to another. Residents and their relatives then complain and she doesn't look so perfect then. And she hasn't a clue who is doing it!"

"So why do you need the wheelchair then?"

"To hide things as I move them about."

"You are wicked!" I couldn't help but grin at the mayhem Nan was probably causing. I ought to have told her off, but I knew any reprimand would be bounced straight back at me.

"A good one I did the other day. Old big head came into the lounge and put her glasses down on the windowsill. As quick as you like I whipped them off and left them on another windowsill out in the corridor. Do you think I will drive her mad?"

"She'll be mad at you if she catches you!" I joked.

Before Nan resumed her narration, I told her about my visit to the museum and suggested we drop-in next time we were out. Nan was agreeable to this and was keenly interested when I drew out the five photographs I had printed.

"This one is of the Orange Tree in 1926, so you would have been eight years old then."

Nan looked at the photograph which showed about 50 locals pictured outside the then thatched roof building, about to embark on a day trip to the coast.

"Look at how smart the men are. Every one of them in a suit, and the girls with their little bonnets." Nan remarked.

"Did you go on the trip?"

"No, I don't think so."

"Do you recognise anyone in the photograph?"

Nan studied the print carefully and raised the photograph closer to her face.

"I know him. And her. What was her name?"

Since the photograph was taken 85 years ago, it was not surprising that Nan couldn't quite recall any names. Looking at the photograph, it amazed me how rapidly the social fabric of the UK had changed so much over the last 100 years, and how Nan had lived through these remarkable times. Several notices were posted on the front of the building, one advertising 'Allotments for rent'. Nowadays any notice is likely to read 'Parking for patrons only.'

The second photograph of the original Baldock Picture House and café shows a part of Baldock long since demolished, today replaced by modern flats.

"This is where you, Di and Brigitte went to the pictures then."

"Yes, look at the poster. Next week 'The Gold Diggers' in 'Natural Colour'. I can't remember going to see that one."

Nan looked at the remaining three photographs.

"Next time we go out, we'll take the photos with us and visit them, and see how much they've changed." I suggested.

"Yes, that's a good idea. I'd like to do that."

1940-41

By early spring of 1940, Mabel had completed all of her training. She was a most dedicated student who had excelled in all categories of her training, and was now proficient in shooting a firearm, jumping from an aircraft with a parachute, sending a message via a radio, following a person of interest, and breaking into a building – among other things. She now sat outside the office of her commanding officer waiting to be given her first assignment. Mabel recalled the first day she had arrived at training camp and sat outside the very same office, and how overwhelmed she felt. In the preceding four months her confidence had flourished, but even so she still felt nervous as she waited to be admitted once again.

Major Ernest Bartlett was a tall thin man who spoke quietly but clearly. He had a reputation for looking after his recruits, and his caring manner had immediately made Mabel feel at ease from the moment she had been introduced to him.

"Congratulations Miss Ellis, these reports are excellent," smiled Bartlett, placing a number of fawn-coloured paper foolscap files on his desk.

"Your first assignment then," Bartlett paused and smiled once again before continuing, "is an unusual one, but of utmost importance. One of the things we do is to help support and maintain escape lines in Belgium and France so that shot-down pilots, VIPs and other persons of interest can make their way back to these shores. This has worked very well to date, but more recently, in the last two months, our success rate has dropped significantly. More worryingly, it is those individuals whom we most want back who are the ones being caught by the Germans. So, either someone is betraying us, or there has been an infiltration along the line. Whoever it is, they are being very clever. We have tightened security, limited the amount of information being shared, varied our escape routes, and even set the odd trap to flush them out, but to no avail. So, you must trust no one."

Mabel nodded as Bartlett picked up another file and opened it.

"So as a French speaker, you are going to France to flush out this informer or infiltrator."

Mabel recalled her very first interview with Major Bartlett, appearing gobsmacked when he read through her file which contained the information that she spoke French. This time she did not betray any surprise, but was still extremely curious as to how they had obtained this piece of information. Brigitte had taught her how to speak the language, but Mabel had only ever told one other person; her sister Di, through her correspondence by letter. She wondered if her letters had been intercepted, or was there a third person who knew?

"Your cover is here in this file, which I will leave with you to learn. Your name will be Nadine Bertrand, a 23-year-old rep working for the Rouen Agricultural Chemical Company. Your boss is a Mr Cedric Duhamel, a very well-respected businessman who works for both us and the Nazis, but naturally his allegiance is with us. Much of his business is now providing chemicals to the Nazis for non-agricultural purposes, but even they realise their troops need to be fed, so a limited number of fertilisers are still produced.

"You will be staying with your cousin Alain Bertrand in a small town outside Paris. He is a farmer and provides produce to the local restaurants, as well as working for us. You also have a sister, Marie-Claire Bertrand, who left Paris to help out her cousin on his farm. Alain Bertrand does have, or did have I should say, two cousins named Nadine and Marie-Claire, but they were both killed in a bombing raid on Paris, so you will take the identity of the younger sister. By the way, the part of your older sister, Marie-Claire, is played by your own sister Di."

Bartlett paused, permitting a small grin to appear at the edges of his mouth, and allowing Mabel time to absorb this revelation. So, Di also worked for Major Bartlett and that's how he knew she spoke French. A desire to ask many questions was burning away inside her, but she knew it would not have been a very professional thing to do. She would find out at a later date.

"Your main task will be to shadow those running the escape line, rather than actually be part of it. This will be very difficult since all our people are trained to spot tails. General

Peters will brief you in detail when you leave here. Di will also be very useful to you. She is our radio operator for the area, and probably knows more about the escape line than any other person in France. However, for security purposes there is much she doesn't know and you will have to discover a lot of things for yourself for much of the time. Your job selling fertilisers will give you the freedom to roam around large areas of the countryside and observe what is going on.

"Your cousin Alain is also a useful pair of eyes since his occupation also gives him licence to move about without generating suspicion. You will report back direct to us using the radio which you know how to use, and if you need to discuss anything out in France, use your sister. For all intents and purposes, you are a saboteur working to bring down the German occupation. My biggest piece of advice to you is to trust no one. Do you have any questions?"

Mabel could think of many questions she wanted to ask, but considered most of them inappropriate despite Major Bartlett's kindly manner. She would instead ask General Peters during their briefing.

"No not really, when do I leave?"

"Two days' time, as long as the weather conditions are favourable. I wish you the very best of luck Miss Ellis. I have every confidence in your ability and that you will make a significant contribution to the war effort. You are a brave young lady."

Major Bartlett stood to signal the end of the meeting, shook Mabel's hand and called for his secretary to take her to General Peters.

The heavy drone of the Lancaster began to dim as it descended beneath the broken clouds and closer to the French countryside. The meeting with General Peters had been a lengthy one. Mabel's job would be to pick up the escape line in the Paris suburbs and follow it to the central city of Tours. Once she was familiar with the route and those involved, she could then snoop around under the pretence of selling fertiliser. It did seem a huge area to cover, especially with the unreliability of the train service as a result of saboteurs, air raids and general shortages. She would do her best though, even if she did feel it was like searching for that proverbial needle in a haystack.

She knew it wouldn't be long now. With the weight of her parachute pack on her back, she realised that the mission and her life could soon be over. She only hoped that the RAF had navigated their path accurately. She didn't particularly want to be trekking in open and unfamiliar countryside for too long. Her documents would justify her being in a number of areas but she didn't want to push her luck this early in the assignment.

The aircraft door slid sideways and the screech of rushing air enveloped her whole body, violently smashing any loose straps against the aircraft's fuselage. The time had come; all of a sudden it dawned on Mabel how fragile life was. She tried to put out of mind the occasion when she had found a saboteur cutting the parachutes at the FFHC. She would be fine though; she had stopped that. Before she had any more time to consider what could happen the order came,

"Jump."

Mabel jumped out into the dark chasm of the night and began to free fall, the cold air blasting across her face. She quickly pulled the ripcord and thankfully the parachute appeared to eject safely as the dome-shaped canopy floated above her, and at once started to slow her descent. The thinning cloud allowed her to focus increasingly on the ground below, as shafts of moonlight highlighted features on the black mass that lay beneath her.

Although Mabel had practised countless night landings back home in the UK as part of her training, each of those were in a controlled environment where a soft even landing was guaranteed. The situation she now found herself in was quite different. If she was really unlucky then she might break a leg, or sprain an ankle. This scenario would place her in danger sooner or later, and the outcome depend heavily on those she would have to seek out for help. Now sensing an increasing proximity to the ground, her heart raced faster as her eyes strained to make out where she would land. The foreboding black mass below started to close in around her as she fell further below the night sky and its stars. Mabel started to prepare her legs for landing. Suddenly her feet and legs made contact with the terrain, not the smoothest landing she had ever made, as she found herself tangled in some form of vegetation.

Fortunately, she didn't turn an ankle on the uneven ground. Once she had come to rest, she instinctively crouched down and remained perfectly still to take in her surroundings. From what Mabel could see she had landed in a farmer's field. She was aware of the pervading smell of the crops and instantly recognised this from her father's own vegetable patch; she had landed in a cabbage field. After a few minutes, satisfied that she had landed unnoticed, Mabel stood up and proceeded to remove the parachute from her back.

Her next task was to successfully hide the parachute. This needed to be done quickly, but also in a location where it wouldn't be found immediately, and initiate a search which would endanger her cover. Mabel was torn between hiding it under the crops, or looking for somewhere else. The latter option could potentially take up valuable time, and would require lugging the heavy parachute and its entrails for some distance. Although she appeared to be in the middle of nowhere, she didn't want to take any unnecessary risks, so she just hoped that the cabbages weren't due to be harvested any time soon.

The night sky was now completely devoid of clouds, allowing the moonlight to pick out a small woodland in the distance, but apart from that, fields of crops stretched out far in front of her.

The RAF's plan was to drop her to the west of Rouen, north of the river Seine. From there she was to pick up either the river or the Caen-to-Rouen railway line and follow one of them into Rouen where she would seek out the offices of the Rouen Agricultural Chemical Company (RACC).

The sky was already beginning to lose its darkness. Her training immediately told her that this was the sun about to rise in the east, and with this information she could quickly ascertain a southerly direction. She wanted to get a good start before dawn broke fully, firstly to put as much distance as possible between her and the parachute, and secondly to put herself in a location that would not raise any questions. If by chance she was found in a location miles away from any settlement, it may spark suspicion.

Without wasting any more time, Mabel carefully made her way to the edge of the field, ever cautious that she didn't tread on any of the crops. She then maintained a brisk pace as she headed in a southerly direction with the ever-brightening horizon to her left. A chorus of songbirds greeting the new day slowly increased in volume as she continued her trek up a long but slight incline. Fortunately, the ground was dry which enabled her to make good progress, and as a result she had now worked up something of a sweat, despite the temperature being only a few degrees above zero on this clear April morning. The emerging sun allowed Mabel to observe her surroundings both in more detail and at a greater distance, but as yet she still hadn't any idea where she was. That was about to change though, as she reached the brow of the steady incline she had been ascending for the best part of the last hour. To her east was a village, in front of her nothing but more fields, and to her west in the distance a vast and continuous area of forest.

Mabel bent down to unfasten her rucksack and removed her French atlas of road maps. After studying the map for a minute or two, she concluded that if the parachute drop had been reasonably accurate, then the forested area could be the Boucles de la Seine National Park to the west of Rouen. She couldn't see any evidence of the river Seine ahead of her though, and the small settlement to her east certainly wasn't Rouen. She scanned the horizon in all directions to look for the imposing edifice of Rouen Cathedral, but the bright low sun on the eastern horizon rendered that task virtually impossible. Finding herself in a quandary was nothing new; should she continue her southerly route or head towards the village? Mabel knew she had to decide quickly before human activity in the area increased and her presence in a farmer's field was noticed. She needed to know where she was and where she was going with some confidence. It was all very well having documents on her that explained her movements, but that would soon be exposed if she was challenged and had no idea where she was.

Acting now with some urgency, Mabel headed towards the village, keeping as close as she could to the hedgerows which lined most of the fields, so that she wasn't easily noticed on any exposed horizons. She was making good progress as the downward projection of the fields enabled her to cover the terrain swiftly. Once or twice, she took the precaution of making a slight detour to avoid any farm buildings and possible encounters with any farmers, or worse still, their dogs.

Once she had neared the settlement, she decided to lie low and observe for a while. It was still early to be going about one's business, but crucially she needed to find out where she was. The place was much larger than she had first thought, probably a small town of about 5000 people at a rough guess. Inching closer to the settlement she could see a road below her leading into the town. After another 15 minutes or so walking, she had reached the road and slid into a dry drainage ditch where she stealthily advanced closer towards the built-up environs. Apart from a couple of farm vehicles, a small van—possibly delivering bread—and a man on a bicycle, there had been very little activity on the road, and certainly no German troops. Eventually, Mabel spotted what appeared to be a name sign for the town. Clambering along the uneven bottomed ditch, she felt a sense of nervous anticipation that the whole success of her mission rested on what was written on this sign.

The initial letter, a 'M' was the first she read, 'M-a-r-o-m-m-e' was the name on the sign. Mabel sat down in the ditch and for the second time drew out her book of maps. Maromme was the settlement immediately due north of Rouen, and it had a railway station. She looked at her watch; it read a quarter to eight. Before entering the station to purchase a train ticket, she decided to buy a copy of Le Monde to add to the authenticity of her pose as a French native. Although she was a stranger to the area, Mabel had good reason to be there and decided to walk into town and find the railway station. Using her well-practised French, she purchased a single to Rouen and was aboard an SNCF service to Paris St Lazare less than ten minutes later. In fact, she needn't have been so nervous, the population appeared to be going about their daily business and didn't seem to pay the slightest attention to a young plainly dressed girl with a rucksack on her back. Disembarking at Rouen, she was able to leave the railway station unchallenged and started out on the walk to the RACC. The city itself was bustling with people making their journeys to work during the morning rush hour. The German occupation was in evidence with a number of tanks and foot patrols strategically placed along the streets.

Mabel marched confidently and determinedly along one of the main arteries that spread out from the station. Once she had crossed the River Seine, Mabel found herself on the Rue du Gros Horlope, Rouen's main thoroughfare. At one end was the city's impressive Gothic cathedral, and at the other, the Place du Vieux Marché which Mabel had discovered during her pre-expedition research and planning was the place where 19-year-old Joan of Arc was burned at the stake for heresy in 1431. The dual thoughts of heroism and death lingered in

Mabel's mind, possibly hoping for a little of the first, but definitely none of the latter. The city streets, with their half-timbered houses reminded her of some of the buildings back home in Baldock. Mabel continued walking in a northerly trajectory as she moved further out from the city centre.

Her entrance into France had so far been undetected. Major Bartlett had purposely only informed General Peters and Cedric Duhamel, the factory owner of his plan. Even her sister would know of her arrival only a few hours before. Although Bartlett did not for one minute suspect her sister of being the traitor for one minute, limiting the number of people and staggering when they were informed, was good practice.

Mabel smelt the RACC before she saw it. The acrid smell of the air made her feel slightly nauseous, and she was glad to be inside the office area gaining respite from the pungency.

After introducing herself to the receptionist as the new sales representative, Mabel was shown into Mr Duhamel's office.

"Glad to have you Miss Ellis," Mr Duhamel greeted her in perfect English, "I trust your journey here was not too difficult?"

Mabel explained that she had been fortunate to have landed close by. Once the formalities were over, Duhamel got down to business and gave her his own personal insight into the fertiliser industry. Mabel was grateful to gain this extra insight. Although she had been briefed extensively back in the UK, she knew if her mission was to succeed, she needed to live and breathe fertiliser, and Duhamel was the one to inject that passion into her. He had started his business from scratch and knew exactly what the average French farmer wanted from a good sales rep.

The logistics of the next 24 hours would enable Mabel to meet up with her sister at her new home in Artenay, a small-town south-west of Paris, just north of Orleans. One of the firm's drivers was delivering a batch of fertiliser to an outlet in Orleans, as well as the newest rep of the RACC. Mabel slept through most of the journey, but for the periods she was awake she conversed in French. The driver, who wasn't a secret agent, was seemingly unaware that Mabel was in fact English, so polished had her accent become.

During World War Two, Artenay's population numbered just over 1100. It's situation on the main Paris to Orléans route meant that it was typically bustling, particularly on market day. Furthermore, the Paris to Tours railway served the town which made it an ideal base for Mabel's assignment. In many ways Artenay was very similar to Baldock; main road to the capital running through it, railway station, church and numerous shops including several bakers, butchers and greengrocers.

Alain Bertrand's farm was a short distance from the edge of town. Mabel had imagined a large grand residence, so she was both shocked and disappointed to find that a ramshackle collection of fairly dilapidated stone farm buildings greeted her. All looked barely habitable, and even though they were constructed of different material than those back home, it reminded her a bit of Hell's End, the slum housing which backed onto the railway in Baldock.

"Hello, is anyone home?" Mabel called out in French, the language she would converse in at all times, except for her intimate chats with Di.

"Nadine, I'm here." Di, or Marie-Claire as Mabel would call her now, appeared from one the outbuildings carrying a basket of assorted produce. Both women advanced towards each other, before putting down what they were carrying, and warmly embracing each other.

"I've missed you, Mabel."

"Me too," replied Mabel, wiping a tear from her eye.

"How are Mum and Dad?" asked Di, also finding the occasion very emotional.

"They're both well. Working very hard as usual. I miss them already."

"Me too. Hopefully this war will be over soon and we'll be back to see them. Anyway, let's get you in and sorted. You must want to wash and change, and have some food."

Di led Mabel into one of the other stone buildings which turned out to be the farmhouse. It was larger than the house back in Baldock which only exaggerated the sparseness of the furnishings, although the dying embers of a couple of logs in the open fire gave the room an unexpected, pleasant warmth.

"I've some nice vegetable stew on the stove and bread baking in the oven. It's very basic here, but you'll be well fed and kept warm. It can still be cold at night on clear days, but the temperature creeps up quite nicely during the day. Let me show you to your room."

Di led Mabel up a set of narrow and steep wooden stairs, which reminded her of climbing a ladder. The room was bare except for the bed and a small closet. The one window looked out over the driveway she had walked up a little over 20 minutes before.

After she had eaten her hearty lunch, Di took Mabel on a tour of the farm. They were just about self-sufficient in every means. One of the outhouses had been converted into a hen house which provided a lucrative side-line with the restaurants in nearby Orleans. The land closest to the house contained goats for milking and was separated from a number of fruit trees. This area was tended by Di, while Alain farmed the fields further out for vegetables and cereals. A small river at the far boundary of the property even provided the odd fish to eat. At the moment food was plentiful, but none of them knew what pressures might be forced upon them as the German war machine swept across France in ever greater numbers.

"I'm really impressed with all the fruit and veg you are growing," Mabel complimented her sister on her efforts.

"Well, we have father to thank for that. All those long boring hours at his allotment have paid off!"

The two sisters laughed, recalling the many tedious jobs that they had performed at the family allotment. Both sisters were happy to spend the afternoon reliving childhood memories of being together and enjoying each other's company, relaxing and sharing those carefree moments from their youth. Taking advantage of the glorious late April sunshine, the sisters had decided to spend the next few hours sun-bathing next to the river. Neither seemed particularly willing to discuss the war just yet, and instead reminisced about the good times spent growing up in Baldock, and owning up to the occasional naughty thing they had done and got away with. Mabel recalled her night of adventure that never quite got off the ground when she attempted to creep out and meet Brigitte.

Di laughed until she almost cried. "Well, who would have thought goody-two shoes Mabel would have done that? Dad would have killed you had he found out."

Mabel looked a little sheepish, perhaps not appreciating being thus labelled.

"Anyway, you did much better the second time I heard. At the FFHC."

"Yes, I did," reflected Mabel, "so how come you ended up here? And doing this sort of stuff?"

"You can blame Eddie for that. I couldn't tell you in my letters at the time, but he had to leave the RAF on medical grounds, and so he started to work for Intelligence. I thought he was still working for the RAF until he tried to sign me up!"

"And then you did the same for me?"

"Not guilty there. Eddie told me the factory manager at the FFHC was so impressed with your actions that he recommended you. Once they started background checks they realised I was your sister. I only told them that you were fluent in French."

"So, are you fluent as well?" Mabel enquired.

"Yes, I would have told you in my letters, but they are heavily checked by the censors for security purposes."

"So where did you learn to speak French?"

"I picked a little up working at the convent. The French nuns were very good at issuing orders! I never used it at home because I'm not sure father would have approved. But I didn't become fluent until I moved to Gloucester. Eddie's older brother John fought at the Somme and married a French girl, Marianne. Being new to Gloucester she befriended me and became a very good friend as well as a sister-in-law. We were talking one day and I mentioned working at the old convent. It just happened from there really. It was good fun learning a new language. I had no idea where it would eventually lead me!"

"So where is Eddie now?"

"He's based in London. What about HRH?"

"He's in northern France somewhere. I haven't seen him for over two months now."

The warmth of the late April sunshine lingered long into the afternoon. Occasionally a dragonfly would buzz past them as it navigated its flight path. Mabel eyed the tranquil river with its green carpet of watercress and invitingly clear water. She was tempted by the idea of a quick dip, even though the water temperature would undoubtedly be somewhat icy this early in the year. Mabel shifted her sun-drenched body so she was looking skywards; the unbroken clear blue vista only interrupted by a few fluttering birds made it almost impossible to believe a war was raging across the continent.

Mabel broke the silence, "I could lay here forever Di."

"Yes, it is rather lovely. We are fortunate to be far from the fronts here. Shall we go for a swim?"

Mabel obviously had no bathing costume with her, nor did Di for that matter, but after some persuasion was encouraged to go skinny dipping. The two sisters happily splashed around in the cool waters seemingly without a care in the world. Sometime later after both had dried off in front of the rapidly sinking sun, they started to walk back to the farmhouse.

"You can help me make dinner Mabel. Then Alain should be back, and after dinner we can help you prepare for your work."

Alain Bertrand was a good deal older than Mabel, probably at least ten years if not more, but his boyish good looks were still very much in evidence. His heavily tanned skin, from many years of working outside, complemented his long brown flowing hair. Mabel felt slightly disloyal to her own husband as her eyes lingered on his muscular form.

Both of Alain's parents were dead so he was in sole charge of the farm. His father had died two years previously from a fall while trying to repair the roof on one of the outhouses. It had been an incredibly difficult time for him, especially since he had lost his mother to cancer as a young child. When the Germans invaded France, Alain felt compelled to join a local resistance group in honour of his parents, to do whatever he possibly could to prevent the farm from falling into the hands of the invader. Since then, he had been recruited by the British to help their cause. In respect of this each morning Alain would deliver farm produce to a number of restaurants around Artenay and beyond to Orléans, which enabled him to receive information, pass on messages, and help with the escape line. Di was the radio operator and contact with England for this stretch of the line.

Di started the discussion after dinner.

"As you know, you are investigating the escape line from Paris to Tours. At the moment most aircrew come down to the north of Paris and are squirreled away as quickly as possible in a number of different safe houses in the capital. All trains for Tours leave Paris from Austerlitz station, but often the aircrew will join the train in the suburbs or just outside Paris. It is safer that way."

Mabel nodded; she hadn't heard any new information yet, but was grateful to hear the arrangements again. She knew that she could have an in-depth discussion with her sister without feeling conscious of making any of the foolish remarks that she had been worried about making in front of Major Bartlett and General Peters.

"I've looked through my notes and the first station that all aircrew have passed through is Étampes. Étampes is a medium-sized town 20 miles south of Paris. From there the train travels south-west to Orléans stopping at a number of smaller stations including here at Artenay. When we send aircrew down the line, the idea is to get rid of them as quickly as possible all the way to the Spanish border, but increasingly the line is being disrupted. This can be due to delays, cancellations and saboteurs. Therefore, we have contacts in most places along the line, so we can hide aircrew quickly should the need arise. Personally, I don't think the infiltrator is beyond Orléans, so I would leave the Orléans to Tours part of the line for now. Alain, you agree?"

"Yes, I do. I think it makes perfect sense. Once the aircrew are being taken down the line, the Germans can nab them anywhere. Most have been captured south of here, and south of Orléans."

Mabel was perhaps a little surprised that Alain seemed to know so much. The emphasis back in England had been on keeping everything under wraps, but on reflection it made perfect sense that Di had someone to discuss strategy and any problems with. Mabel asked her first question.

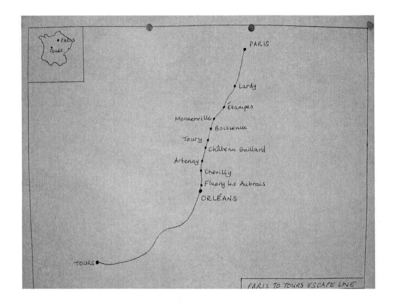

PARIS

Lardy

Étampes

Monnerville

Boissenux

Toury

Château Gaillard

Artenay

Chevilly

Fleury les Aubrais

ORLÉANS

TOURS

PARIS TO TOURS ESCAPE LINE

"So do you have any hunches or gut feelings where your leak is?"

Di looked at Alain again, who continued with a shake of the head.

"No, all those involved are good people, all loyal French patriots. I'm sure it's nobody in this area, but then others will feel the same along their part of the line. It's a mystery. You will have a big advantage over us though in that nobody knows who you are, and nobody else apart from us three knows London has suspicions."

Not surprisingly neither Di nor Alain could provide any likely leads; this, after all, was why she had been assigned here because other investigations had hit a brick wall. Mabel listened keenly as Alain provided detailed profiles of some of the line's operatives that he had contact with. She began to appreciate just how difficult her task was going to be.

*

I could sense that Nan had quite a story to tell of her time in France, but she was tired now, and I knew that I had to be patient and wait till another time to hear the next instalment.

I rose from the chair and was just as I was about to leave, when there was a knock-on Nan's door and Mrs Caunter appeared in the doorway.

"Can I just have a quiet word please?"

Before I could reply she was at my side and lowering her normally glass-shattering voice to a whisper as if she was about to divulge some top-secret information.

"I don't want to alarm you, but has Mabel had any items go missing or perhaps turned up where they are not supposed to be?"

"No, I don't think so, what sort of items?"

Before Mrs Caunter could answer, Nan interjected.

"My red dressing gown has gone missing."

"You didn't say," I replied.

"Well, I'm sure it will turn up."

I turned back to Mrs Caunter.

"What's going on then?"

"It's nothing to worry about. One of the residents seems to be taking things and then leaving them in different places. We haven't a thief here, just someone a bit forgetful. Please let me know if you see anything, and I'll have a look for Mabel's dressing gown."

"I will." I nodded.

Once Mrs Caunter had left us, I gave Nan my best disbelieving look.

"So have you really lost your dressing gown?"

Nan laughed, "No, just covering my tracks like any good spy would!"

"I thought so, but tell me how did you know she asked me about the missing items? She whispered it to me, and you can't hear that well. I don't think you've covered your tracks that well!"

Nan grinned, "She's too stupid to realise that. And anyway, I don't know why she always has to ask the family if everything is all right. Why can't she ask me directly? I'm just a bit dodgy on my pegs, not in my mind. That woman is all for show."

"She's probably frightened of you!"

"Rubbish. She just likes to look good in front of visitors, and to gather comments on what a grand job she's doing. Total big-head."

"Yes, I'm sure you are right."

Chapter 4

Several days of increasingly sultry and sticky weather had elapsed giving way to a prolonged period of thunderstorms. Thereafter clear and sunny skies had resumed, albeit with slightly cooler temperatures thanks to a northerly air flow. Since it was Wednesday, I thought it would be an ideal day to take Nan to Baldock Museum. Run by a small group of volunteers, the museum only opens on Sundays and Wednesdays, and on special occasions such as the Baldock May Street fair.

"I thought we were going to visit the places in the photos today?" Nan replied when I told her that we were going to the museum.

"There is a bit of a wind today, so it might be best to go to the museum." I suggested, instantly realising that the mere mention of any negative climatic words would place in jeopardy any venturing outside.

"It's cold out then?"

"No, in the sun it is fine. It's just that some of these places might be in the shade. We'll go to the museum today. Has Mrs Caunter caught you moving things yet?" I asked, quickly changing the subject.

"No of course not, but I have a special surprise for her today!" Nan looked down at her wristwatch, "and I need to be back here in time for afternoon tea."

A forlorn look of resignation spread across my face. Shaking my head, I said, "Don't tell me."

"I'll tell you when we get to my room."

Nan was certainly excited about something, and I didn't especially want to know, but I knew that I would have to humour her.

"So, what have you done now?" I asked once we were safely in the confines of her room away from any residents with especially acute hearing.

"Well, I've taken Pauline's mug from the tea tray and put it in Mrs Caunter's office. She'll be furious when she finds out!"

Pauline was perhaps the most awkward of Nan's fellow residents. She always insisted on sitting in the same chair in the communal lounge and would wear a terrifying glare, or even tell anyone who had the audacity to sit in her chair to move – in no uncertain terms. Nan disliked her almost as much as Mrs Caunter. I had to laugh. The very thought of Pauline and Mrs Caunter battling it out was highly amusing. I grinned, before helping Nan get ready. In anticipation of her inevitable moaning about it being cold out, I tucked an extra blanket down the back of the wheelchair before setting off.

Wednesday was market day, and had been so in Baldock since at least the 16th century. As a young boy I could remember virtually the whole length of the High Street being lined with market stalls, probably in excess of 30. In Nan's time livestock was traded too. Sadly, the market today typically numbers less than five stalls, a demise largely induced by the arrival of the Tesco superstore which opened on the old Kayser Bondor site in the mid-1980s.

Inside the museum I guided Nan into the storeroom-cum-research room where the many collections of photographs were kept.

"It's cold in here." Nan grumbled.

Mr Miles, one of the curators, must have heard from the adjacent room since he appeared in the doorway with a small plug-in fire.

"Is this of any use?" he enquired, with a wide grin on his face.

We all laughed, and thanked him as he bent down and plugged the appliance into the wall socket.

"Heating on in June, I don't know!" I joked.

Nan typically chose to be extra deaf at that moment and opened the album of Kayser Bondor photographs. There were a few prints from before the war when it was still known as the Full Fashion Hosiery Company, including a 1938 snap of the Christmas party.

"You must be in this one somewhere?" I asked.

"I doubt it. I have never liked having my photo taken."

Nan was right, she wasn't in the photograph. Another photograph dating from March 1946 showed Queen Mary and a young Princess Elizabeth being escorted around the premises. Nan commented on how lovely the future queen looked. As a true Royalist, I'm sure Nan would have been disappointed to have missed out on that day, having been at home with her firstborn.

"Look at that," Nan pointed to another photograph. "That's the dispatch room. There at the back is the hatch I climbed through when I apprehended that girl that night."

I admired the photograph, sensing how pleased Nan was in reliving these moments from her youth.

Back outside in the fresh air we found a sheltered seat by the new war memorial which faced up the High Street. One of the widest in the country, the High Street still retains much of its history and charm. I sat for a few moments considering the many stories the street could yield from centuries past, before Nan resumed the next part of her narration.

1941

Days passed slowly as Mabel began to settle in on the farm. While she was enjoying the relaxing and carefree atmosphere of living in the French countryside, Mabel was in truth itching to get involved in the work. She had considered paying visits to a number of the addresses that Di and Alain had provided her with under the pretence of selling fertiliser, but decided against this on the grounds that she may need to visit some of these properties at a later date, and she didn't want to risk being recognised and end up blowing her cover. She would just need to be patient and wait for Di to inform her when some aircrew would be sent down the escape line. In the meantime, she studied her notes and the list of stations which served the area she would first focus on. The list read:

Étampes
Monnerville
Boisseaux
Toury
Château Gaillard
Artenay
Chevilly

Fluery les Aubrais
Orléans

It made sense to focus on Étampes first and then follow the line southwards.

Mabel's investigation started properly a few days later when Di received notification that three aircrew were to be sent down the line. She would travel up to Étampes the very next morning and be in place to trail the group of aircrews as they arrived in Étampes and were transferred to a different escort, who would take them as far as Tours or beyond if all went well. Di went over the plan that London had agreed.

Mabel would follow and observe the party from a distance and report back any suspicious behaviour. She wasn't that convinced that this was the plan most likely to yield results, as it seemed an awful lot of travelling for ultimately little reward. She was of the opinion that she needed to get closer to those involved in the escape line.

Travelling with an overnight bag and a small attaché case of RACC paperwork, Alain had dropped her off at Artenay station for the 08.10 train to Paris. On arriving in Étampes she would have the remainder of the day to familiarise herself with the town. The train journey was not a rapid one, causing Mabel to stare through the dirty window at the verdant and lush countryside, while constantly considering other methods she could employ to expose the infiltrator.

Before the train had arrived at Étampes, Mabel had formulated an alternative plan. She was aware that the escort would be very vigilant and on the lookout for any tails at the station so she decided that she would join the train not at Étampes, but two stops further up the line at Lardy. Lardy was a smaller place than Étampes, but she managed to find a room in a small run-down hotel close to the station. Once she was booked in and safely in her bedroom, she sat down on the bed and opened the small attaché case. She knew that she needed to make a couple of calls to farmers in the area before nightfall, just in case any random checks were carried out by the Germans, but firstly she wanted to check train times for tomorrow. Di was unable to provide her with any exact train times for the aircrew the next day. This was another small precaution London insisted on to ensure the capture of aircrews by the enemy was made that much harder. In fact, not even London knew which train service they would be using, having left it up to the individual handler to decide. Timings, and the subsequent messages to other escorts, were invariably left until the last minute. That way everyone felt a little safer – if that was of course possible given the dangerous work they all selflessly undertook.

Mabel had identified two morning trains from Paris to Tours that the aircrew would probably travel on. The early-morning train would be busy and provide good cover but the Germans would also be more likely to carry out random checks on a crowded train with a greater probability of finding illegal activity. Mabel decided that she would board the early-morning train at Lardy, departing at 0810, and try to identify the party of aircrew. If they were not aboard, then she would alight at the next stop, Chamarande and wait for the next train, the 0920. If this happened, she would again seek to identify the aircrew as the train travelled towards the next stop of Étampes. The benefit of this plan was to identify the aircrew before their new escort picked them up. That way, Mabel thought her presence would be less noticeable and therefore enable her to get closer to the group.

She didn't enjoy a particularly sound night's sleep; the bed was soft and springy, and she lay awake running through her plan over and over again. The next morning, Mabel felt slightly tired but not overly concerned as the excitement of the day would carry her through whatever lay ahead. She had looked forward to this day ever since she had arrived at the farmhouse at Artenay, so a poor night's sleep would not hold her back in any way. After purchasing a single ticket, Mabel walked along the platform working out where she thought the first carriage would stop. Once the train had stopped, she would board the carriage and then walk through it pretending to look for somewhere to sit, and at the same time hopefully observe where the three aircrew were sitting. If she had been in England, she would have been able to see easily into the carriages as the train arrived in the station, but here in France the trains were much higher with the seating compartments well above the eye line.

Mabel checked the station clock, five minutes past eight, and rather surprisingly only three other people stood waiting on the platform. Nearest to her were a woman and a boy approximately eight years old, who Mabel took to be her son. Dressed in a smart blue school uniform, the boy waited patiently with the woman. The only other passenger was a middle-aged businessman carrying a black leather briefcase. At ten past eight the train, puffing plumes of dense grey smoke, appeared at the top of the bend about 500m north of the station. Almost simultaneously, about a dozen other passengers suddenly appeared on the platform beside her. These seasoned travellers obviously knew exactly when to arrive for the train, at 0813 to be precise. Perhaps they had been waiting elsewhere.

By the time the train was slowly hauling itself out of the station, Mabel was already walking along the corridor of the first carriage, idly glancing into the compartments as she moved down the train. The train was not as busy as she had expected, so she decided to change tack and give the impression she was looking for a friend to avoid any unwelcome offers of a seat. Furthermore, this would allow her to inspect her fellow passengers a few seconds longer.

Most of the passengers she had observed so far were a mixture of businessmen and casual labourers. Once or twice, she felt the urge to pause and check certain passengers more carefully but she knew this was not feasible. The fact that the train consisted of compartments rather than being open-plan played into her strategy. Mabel knew that the guide would, in all likelihood, be sitting in the same compartment as the aircrew. Midway through the third carriage, she felt sure she had her prey in sight.

Three casually-dressed labourers sat looking out of the window, while a young girl, probably the same age as Mabel, sat by the door next to the corridor. Mabel quickly walked on by and entered the next compartment. The young boy with his mother, who had been waiting with her on the platform at Lardy, were both seated along with two businessmen who were in conversation with each other. The mother looked up and smiled at Mabel, who returned the compliment. Having positioned herself by the door facing up the corridor, Mabel would hopefully see the guide leave at Étampes in two stops time.

Initially Mabel's bold plan was to leave her own compartment at Étampes and move into the one next door holding the three possible aircrew once the first guide had left. She realised that this was a ridiculous idea though, as later she planned to follow the guide back to Étampes, which would have been suicidal had she sat with them on the entire journey to Orléans and allowed the guide to become familiar with her appearance. By not doing this, she had been much cleverer, as she was already on the train when the next guide took over. Had she sat herself in the next compartment, she would have in all likelihood discovered very little that would help unmask any infiltrator.

Mabel had brought a paperback novel with her, so that at key moments she would make out she was reading it to reduce the risk of any of her fellow passengers distracting her. She needed to keep a keen eye on events in the corridor ahead of her.

At Étampes, the young girl in the next compartment vacated the train. For a few seconds Mabel considered following her, but realised she had to be patient and follow one lead at a time. It did occur to her that the young girl could be outside the station by now telephoning the authorities and informing them of the whereabouts of the three young aircrew.

Shortly another girl entered the compartment beyond Mabel's, so she felt sure she had called this correctly, and that next door were the three aircrew. The train departed Étampes three minutes late, and continued its journey southwards stopping fairly frequently at what seemed to be identical stations, such was the lack of variation in both the natural and human landscape. Even though Mabel was on her first assignment, the time began to drag as the monotony of the journey began to take hold. She kept a mental list of the stations the train was to stop at, the last one having been Chevilly, and now she assumed the train was slowing down as it approached what should be Fleury les Aubrais, the last stop before Orléans.

As the locomotive slowly eased into the station, Mabel immediately knew something was wrong; a long line of German soldiers on the platform instantly set her heart racing. The lead officer barked instructions to his subordinates who marched quickly to all exits of the train and started to empty the carriages of passengers. Mabel lingered for as long as she could, since she wanted to follow and stay close to the aircrew. Once all the passengers had been cleared from the train, some soldiers were sent back on board either to check it was empty or to conduct a search. Mabel wasn't sure which, but it was clear they were acting on some form of intelligence.

Down on the platform the passengers were made to form a long line as a number of tables were dragged from the railway station office to form a makeshift search area. Each passenger was prompted to move forward and present any belongings they were carrying in order for them to be searched. Passports and papers were also being checked.

The guide had ensured there was a distance of about half a dozen people between herself and the aircrew. This was common procedure since the very last thing the escape line needed was for one of its members to be captured, questioned and ultimately tortured by the Gestapo. The guide was keeping her head down, looking towards the front of the line. All of this seemed standard practice; Mabel wondered if the aircrew were about to be exposed and captured. She also questioned the wisdom of putting herself next in the line behind the aircrew. Was her fledgling career as a spy about to become a cropper on her very first mission?

The guide had just had her papers and belongings checked, and was now waiting behind the makeshift checkpoint. One of the aircrews was becoming distinctly fidgety, his head twisting and turning in all directions as his eyes desperately sought an escape route. The German machine guns on display rendered this impossible, but it became increasingly apparent he would try to make a futile escape attempt.

Mabel faced a difficult dilemma here, should she let him run and be killed (with the added possibility of her close proximity encouraging the Germans to assume she was attached to him), or should she chance an even riskier strategy with a potentially better outcome? Mabel hadn't entered this position by being timid, so she opted for the latter.

Quickly seizing the airman's left hand, she whispered to him,

"You'll be fine. Trust me."

The airman froze momentarily before glancing sideways at her in amazement.

"They're not looking for you. Why would they check everyone if they are just looking for aircrew? Think about it."

The airman processed Mabel's words and appeared to concur with what she had said. They were now two persons back from the checkpoint. Suddenly two German soldiers, on the orders of a superior, grabbed the man whose belongings were currently being searched. He was swiftly marched off the platform and through the station building, probably into a waiting truck. The German officer slammed the man's small brown suitcase shut and followed him. His accompanying officer screamed orders for everyone to get back on the train.

Without any further conversation, Mabel left the airman and made her way back to the same compartment as before. She had no idea if the guide had seen her intervention or whether the airman would inform her. If the compartment housed other passengers, then he may not get the opportunity. In the event of Mabel's cover being blown then she wouldn't be able to follow the guide back to Étampes. Regardless of what happened next, Mabel was very content to know that she had almost certainly saved the life of one young airman. Perhaps he would get back to England and fly many successful sorties and help win the war.

Mabel had made up her mind to exit the train as quickly as possible once it had reached Tours. She knew that tailing the aircrew would be fairly impossible now; at least one of the three men knew her face and in all probability the guide did too. Deliberately moving down the carriage, Mabel was one of the first passengers to position herself by the exit as the train slowed on its approach to Tours station. She avoided looking over her shoulder to see if the aircrew were out in the corridor yet, hoping that they were unaware of her presence. As soon as the train had stopped, she lowered herself down from the carriage and marched purposefully towards the exit.

Leaving the station, she quickly scanned the Boulevard HauteLook, before crossing the road and entering one of the many bars which lined the street. On entering the bar, Mabel noticed the whole of the back wall was covered with mirror panels. Rather than try to observe the aircrew from the bar window, and run the risk of being observed, she moved towards the back of the bar and pretended to be viewing the food on offer. Instead, using the mirrors to observe the street, she concentrated on trying to spot the aircrew leaving the station. About ten minutes had elapsed before the aircrew did so. By this time, Mabel was at a table sipping the cup of coffee she had ordered. The young girl who was escorting them, albeit some ten yards ahead, wore the same beige coat, but was most definitely a different girl to the one on the train. Mabel had not been expecting this. It was standard practice that the guide would leave the station along with any aircrew; perhaps something was wrong? She was tempted to follow the aircrew and guide, but her plan was to follow the original guide back to Étampes. Mabel quickly consulted her train timetable to find out if a train to Étampes had already departed. It hadn't, and wouldn't do so for another 40 minutes, if it was on schedule. Therefore, the first girl was most likely still in Tours.

Her first assignment looked like ending up being fairly fruitless in terms of gaining information about the identity of the leak. The aircrew hadn't been betrayed it seemed, so she wondered if this particular guide could be excluded from her investigation. Of course, only certain aircrew and VIPs were being caught. This was the cleverness of it all; keep the escape line open and only take what you need. Perhaps the aircrew were not that important and were allowed to make their way back to England. She did at least have the satisfaction of preventing one, or possibly all three of them, from being captured by the Germans, and for this she was delighted. As the aircrew disappeared beyond the horizon there was nothing else left to do, but to make her way back to Artenay. Before doing so she decided to order an omelette for lunch and another cup of coffee. She really enjoyed her cup of coffee, and wondered if it would become rationed as the war progressed.

After paying the bill, Mabel left the bar and crossed the Boulevard Heuteloup for the train station. On entering the concourse, she checked the departure board and made her way to platform two for the next Paris train. As Mabel stood waiting on the platform, she felt a figure draw up beside her. Without even turning her head she knew instantly it was the guide from the train. Annoyed that she had been careless, Mabel quickly racked her brains for a plan on how she should play this out.

"So, who are you?" the girl asked in a low discreet voice.

"I'm one of you. I'm on the same side." Mabel looked closely at this new guide for the first time. She was certainly no older than her and, like herself, was putting her own safety at great risk for the sake of the war.

"Check with Alain," Mabel added, knowing that her 'cousin' had dealings with many of the guides. This piece of information appeared to provide the girl with some satisfaction.

"Yes, well I suppose you did help us out earlier."

Mabel was beginning to feel some semblance of trust had begun to be established between the two of them, however she was wary of how the conversation should progress.

"I expect I need to brush up on my tailing techniques?" Mabel offered.

"So, you were tailing me?"

"Yes, Alain suggested that I tailed you and the aircrew before my first run."

Mabel hoped that the girl wouldn't contact Alain and expose her lie. She also hoped that her story seemed feasible enough. "It wasn't to test you, but just so I could get used to the procedure."

"So where did you tail me from?"

Mabel decided to tell her questioner the truth, even if it might hurt her pride.

"From Étampes."

"I must be slipping. You are good, I didn't notice you until the search, and then you did the right thing at Tours by leaving first."

"So how did you find me?"

"I knew you would be waiting for me to leave the station so I telephoned another guide to come and fetch the aircrew. Slightly risky but I couldn't take any chances."

"That's why you didn't leave the station immediately then."

"Yes, and once they had left, I waited for you to tail them. Of course, you didn't, and like you I waited in a café ready for your next move."

"Watching me?"

"That's right."

The mid-afternoon train wasn't very busy so the two girls had a compartment to themselves. Mabel had umpteen questions she wanted to ask, but knew that protocol meant that no information should pass between them, especially since they hadn't been cleared by the organisation, although their conversation had probably gone beyond that protocol already. Both the female agents seemed to appreciate this and turned to more general topics of discussion such as hobbies and family details.

Mabel decided to leave the train at the stop beyond Artenay, Château Gaillard, since she didn't want to disclose where she was living. She also felt sure that Alain's address wasn't known so it was to protect him as well, should the girl assume she was staying with him. Mabel waved goodbye to her new colleague who reciprocated, and spoke one last message to her,

"Hope to work with you soon."

Once Mabel had caught the train back to Artenay, she began the short hike back to the farmhouse with a great deal on her mind. She looked up at the clear blue sky which had prevailed for three consecutive days now, and wondered what she would say to Di. She hadn't followed orders on her very first assignment and allowed herself to be identified by one of the guides under suspicion. In her defence, she had almost certainly saved the life of at least one airman. The dilemma was whether to tell the truth and risk Di pulling rank on her, or say nothing and risk being found out the next time Alain happened to see the guide from the train. She knew Di wouldn't deliberately pull rank. Both sisters loved each other dearly, but Mabel didn't want to put Di in a difficult position. Bearing all this in mind, she decided to come clean and tell her older sister exactly what had happened. Mabel felt relieved to get the events out in the open, and even more so when Di reacted positively.

"Don't worry Mabel. It's probably not the start you envisaged, but above all we are here to save the lives of British aircrew, and by the sound of it, you certainly did that today. I'll tell Alain what happened later. He'll be fine with it, so London need not find out."

"What if this girl, Valeria, is the one?"

"Well, it could come down to a process of elimination in the end. The good news is that she doesn't know the true purpose of your visit, nor where you are living either."

Di had always been the most clear-headed and logical member of her family, and today proved no exception.

Mabel had perhaps expected Alain to be a little frosty with her following her slip-up, but quite the opposite was true. He went out of his way to reassure her that things were fine, and even found the time, in between farming and delivering, to advise Mabel on general points she should adhere to during her next assignment. Di certainly could do no wrong in Alain's eyes.

*

"That's amazing Nan. You actually saved their lives, so much for not doing much during the war!"

"Come, it's nearly 4 o'clock." Nan dismissed my praise in typically modest style. "You'll stay for a cup of tea, won't you?"

I could sense that Nan wouldn't take 'No' for an answer, and she desperately wanted me to witness her little set-up.

"Very well," I replied, "I just hope it doesn't go too far."

The rattle of the tea trolley was greeted with enthusiasm by the residents who always looked forward to their afternoon cuppa and accompanying biscuit. Nan took her usual strong tea with pink wafer. Pauline was bent down at the trolley frantically searching the lower shelf for her owl-motif mug. Having been unsuccessful, she straightened herself up, and demanded of the poor unsuspecting kitchen hand where it had disappeared to.

"Where's my mug? What have you done with it? Have you broken it?"

Her directness and continual barrage of questions saw the poor girl flounder, stumbling to find any words, before one of the carers stepped in.

"What is it, Pauline?"

"My mug's gone."

"What does it look like?"

"It's my owl mug. You surely know that."

By this time, the commotion had brought Mrs Caunter herself into the lounge.

"It's just not good enough," Pauline continued.

Nan looked at me and smirked, before whispering, "The best bit is yet to come with any luck."

"Come to my office Pauline and we'll discuss it there." Mrs Caunter suggested, glancing around the room to observe who was watching the disturbance.

"I knew it!" exclaimed Nan triumphantly, "she doesn't want a fuss out here so she's taking her to her office. Now she'll be caught out. Come, let's follow them."

Reluctantly I wheeled Nan out into the corridor and into the vicinity of Mrs Caunter's office. The door was very slightly ajar so we could hear Pauline's raised voice and most of Mrs Caunter's responses.

"That's my mug. What is the meaning of this? You've stolen my mug."

"I... I... I don't know how it got there..."

"Well, you could have at least asked me if you wanted to borrow it. You wait until everybody else hears about this. I bet it's you who's been moving the stuff around."

"I'm very sorry Pauline. I don't know how this could have happened."

After a few more exchanges, a red-faced Pauline exited the office and returned to the lounge.

"Don't you feel guilty?" I asked Nan.

"No, they're both pretentious fools. Anyway, old Bighead won't get into trouble. No one will take any notice of obnoxious Pauline."

Nan was probably right, but I was a little concerned that her mischievous behaviour would be discovered sooner or later.

"The next warm day, we'll go out with the photos." I promised before leaving.

Chapter 5

It was the perfect day to carry out our mini-tour of old Baldock; a clear blue sky, no wind and none of the oppressive humidity we often get during hot spells of weather.

"What happened with Mrs Caunter and Pauline?" I asked as I helped Nan get ready.

"Oh nothing, it's all blown over. I told you that it would. Pauline kept going on about it, but nobody took much notice, only those that are easily led."

"Well, I hope you are going to stop now. You will get caught one of these days."

"Don't worry I have. She's got all the staff nosing around watching everyone, making extra visits to the lounge and stuff. I'm too clever for them. Always a step ahead."

"Well, yes, I suppose so," I agreed with Nan before adding, "you are an ex-spy after all!"

"So, I need to find something else to do."

I was pleased that Nan had not involved herself in any more mischief at Templars. For once I was able to exchange pleasantries with Mrs Caunter without the worry of being asked any embarrassing questions. Although I was more than a little curious about any new plans Nan had formulated to wreak havoc, I decided not to ask.

Our first visit was to the old site of FW Cooper's butcher, which today is occupied by a takeaway joint. Nan removed the corresponding photograph from the envelope and placed it onto her lap where we could both see it to make a comparison. Although the shop frontage was unrecognisable the building above was remarkably similar. The large first-floor bay window with its curved base still survives today. Back in the 1930s a hand-painted cow of intricate detail was displayed on the base. Unfortunately, today it has been covered up with black paint, but the distinctiveness of the window remains. In the photograph a long line of pig carcasses hangs out from the open shop front above the pavement.

"I couldn't imagine that being allowed today with health and safety, and probably too many squeamish people. You didn't mind then?" I asked.

"No, it was commonplace. Everything had to be bought and prepared yourself. No ready meals back then."

Nan pointed at the three butchers who stood proudly at each end of their displayed meats.

"Look at how smart they are. Shirt and ties, and look at their pristine white aprons. The photo must have been taken in the morning for them to be that clean."

Crossing Hitchin Street, we entered Church Street, the road in which Nan was born. Very much gentrified now, the street is one of Baldock's oldest and retains much of its old charm.

We located more or less the exact spot from which the old photograph was taken, and looked down the street with St Mary's church on the left and housing opposite it. The most obvious difference in the 1930s photograph was the large structure which sat at the bottom of the street obstructing the view of the railway line which can be seen clearly today.

"What's that building?" I asked.

"That's the old gas power station. I can remember it as a young girl when I played out in the street, but it was certainly knocked down before the war."

"And no cars," I remarked.

"Yes, it was lovely."

"And look at all the old pubs."

I could make out the pub signs for the Eight Bells, the Bull's Head and the Star.

"Yes, none are left today," commented Nan. I could remember the Bull's Head closing around 1986 when I was 18 years old, but had no recollection of the other two. Baldock St Mary's church has stood since the Reformation and its splendour dominates the town's skyline. It seemed a fitting place to allow Nan to continue her narration, so we found a bench which was not overly shaded by the churchyard's many yew trees.

Before Nan resumed her story, I pointed out a gravestone that had always aroused my curiosity.

George Ellis
Died 1768
Aged 74
Beloved husband of
Mary Ellis
Died 1775
Aged 79
Reunited

"That gravestone there, George Ellis, died exactly 200 years before I was born. Do you know if he was a relative?"

"Not for definite, but I would say it is highly probable. Both George and Mary are family names. My father and grandfather were both called George. It was very common in those days to name the eldest son after the father, and I don't expect there would have been many branches of the Ellis family in Baldock back then."

I used my fingers to work out some quick arithmetic.

"He was born in 1696, so taking roughly 30 years each generation, he would be seven generations back. He would have been your great, great, great, great, great-grandfather!"

"Perhaps you ought to trace our family tree, and find out for sure." Nan suggested.

It was a suggestion I would definitely consider, since local history interested me greatly.

"He lived until he was 74 years old. That's a really good age considering he was born in the 17th century. Perhaps he was wealthy?"

"I believe the family was well-off at one time."

"What happened to it then?"

"Probably gambled away," Nan laughed as she settled down to recommence her narration.

1941

Mabel's second assignment was a success in that she carried it out to the letter, and remained unobserved throughout. In the purpose of gleaning or uncovering some information regarding the leak, it was a disappointment. Essentially, she had spent hours sitting on a train journeying from Étampes to Tours and back, and then following the guide to her home. She knew that a massive slice of luck would be needed to uncover anything. In effect, operations needed a significant tweak.

Mabel had two improvements to suggest when she next sat down with Di and Alain. Firstly, she suggested that they 'set-up' some of the guides by pretending the odd aircrew were important and needed to be returned to England at all costs. This, Mabel thought, could flush out the infiltrator. Secondly, in tandem with her first suggestion, she would need to be positioned in the vicinity when the message was given to the guide. That way she would be able to tail the guides immediately and hopefully identify any passing of information. Both Di and Alain agreed that the plan could work and was worth a try. Inevitably there were a couple of drawbacks. Firstly, it would put the lives of innocent aircrew at risk since it increased their chance of capture, and secondly how would Mabel be able to identify guides without their accompanying aircrew when the telephone call was made. The second problem could be relatively easily solved by providing addresses and detailed descriptions of the guides, but the first problem posed a significant moral quandary. Alain spoke next.

"It will depend on you identifying any suspicions before the aircrew are sent down the line. That obviously won't be possible every time. We can limit the impact by sending just one airman down the line, but it is still one human being. I don't like it, but I think we must give it a try and just hope we strike gold early."

Di and Alain reluctantly agreed to go along with the new plan.

Alain hauled the last few crates of vegetables onto the back of his van. He had some genuine deliveries to make, but the main purpose of his visit to Étampes was to pick up and deliver some messages. Mabel jumped into the cab beside Alain and pulled the door shut. One of the messages Alain was to deliver was to another guide called Lucille. Accompanying Alain had a dual purpose of taking Mabel to the house where Lucille lived, and being able to identify the girl when Alain knocked on the door to deliver the vegetables. For this purpose, Mabel was to vacate the van a few hundred metres before the house so that she could locate herself in an inconspicuous position to observe.

"Isn't this a weakness that all the changeovers occur in Étampes?" Mabel enquired as they drove into the town.

"In a way, but it's the largest place between Paris and Orléans. In a small place stranger are noticed easily, so it's probably the best of a bad lot. Sometimes we can do a straight run from Paris to Tours, but it's getting more difficult with all the different hold-ups."

Alain was referring to the increasing number of checks by the Germans, and the inevitable wartime delays to the trains. Unattached saboteurs were also adding to the problem. He slowed the van as he took a turn from the main street into a busy residential road. Alain quickly issued Mabel with some instructions as to which house, he was visiting and what she needed to do. After Mabel got out of the van, Alain drove on for a few hundred metres and pulled up outside one of the houses. He dragged off one of the crates of vegetables from the back of his truck and banged on the front door. Mabel, walking up on the other side of the road, was not quite parallel with the house when the door opened and Alain swiftly entered. Had she not been looking at that precise moment, or distracted for a second or two, she would have missed the girl. Mabel continued to walk past the house and to the end of the street to find the small park where Alain had told her to wait.

She had been seated for just a couple of minutes when Alain drove past in his truck and parked further up the street. He had explained to Mabel only a few minutes previously that most visits only lasted a matter of seconds so as to give the impression of a bona fide delivery. At the far end of the road Alain turned his van around so it was now facing back down the road towards the centre of Étampes, and parked it at the side of the road next to the park. Mabel quickly jumped in, so that both she and Alain now had a good view of Lucille's house. Alain planned to stay with Mabel for as long as he could since there was no suitable hiding place on the street for Mabel to observe Lucille's house. He knew Lucille had no telephone, so if she was to make contact with the German authorities, she would need to do so by foot that afternoon. The hope was that she would leave her house and make that contact very shortly, since Alain couldn't stay with Mabel indefinitely. Firstly, he had other deliveries to make, and secondly, they couldn't sit in the car watching for any length of time without arousing suspicion.

Fortunately, they didn't have to wait long before Lucille appeared in the doorway of her house. Once she had started walking down the hill towards the town centre, Mabel left Alain to make his other deliveries, and started to pursue the girl along the street. Mabel was aware that Lucille, on more than one occasion, looked behind her to observe if she was being followed. When this happened, Mabel kept her head down, or looked elsewhere. Her training meant that she had already memorised in detail what the girl was wearing. She was confident that if she lost her on entering the town centre, she would have no problem spotting her again. After Lucille had turned left into the main thoroughfare, Mabel quickly took off her coat and expertly stuffed it into her bag. She also gathered her long locks and tied them up into a bun to create a different appearance. On entering the main street Mabel had momentarily lost her prey, but after crossing the road she was able to get a better view of the pedestrian traffic ahead of her. Lucille had stopped by the window of a clothes shop. This was standard practice for the organisation, so that any tails could be flushed out. Almost at the same time Mabel saw a man dressed in a brown overcoat duck into a shop entrance. The possibility struck Mabel that Lucille was being followed, and even more worryingly she wasn't sure that the guide had seen her tail hide in the shop entrance. If this was the case it would be impossible for Mabel to complete her mission without putting herself in danger.

Mabel had got very used to thinking on her feet, and this situation was no different. She too stopped outside a shop and used the window reflection to identify Lucille on the opposite side of the road. Once Lucille started to walk again, she waited to see if her tail followed suit. About ten seconds later the figure followed her. Mabel turned around and watched the two figures advance along the thoroughfare. There were plenty of other shoppers, workers and families on the street so she didn't feel her own position was at risk, but she became convinced that Lucille was being tailed.

Outside a bar, Lucille stopped and waited on the pavement. This time the man in the overcoat had no shop doorway or other hiding place close at hand, so he continued walking past her. At that moment another girl of similar age to Lucille arrived, and both girls embraced. This gave the impression of two friends simply meeting for a coffee and chat. Mabel was convinced of this too; after all, she decided, you would hardly meet in a bar to discuss any sabotage plans.

Mabel lingered briefly to see if the man stopped or met anyone. It was possible he had an accomplice who would now take up the tail, but now that Lucille had stopped walking and entered the bar, it would be difficult to identify anyone. Mabel then made the decision to tail the man. She appreciated that her actions could put her in danger, but if Lucille's cover was compromised then the aircrew due to come under her care tomorrow could end up being captured. Her pursuit lasted just another two minutes as the man mounted the steps of Étampes town hall and entered the building. With the Nazi swastika fluttering atop its flag pole, instead of the tricolour, Mabel was more convinced than ever that Lucille had been followed. She continued walking past the town hall until she came to a convenient stopping point. Mabel entered the bar and ordered a cup of coffee, and thought about what to do next. She could either look for a telephone to warn Di and Alain, or make her way back to Artenay. The first option was the riskier, even if she did find somewhere relatively private to phone from, there was a chance that the line would be tapped. Since she had enough time to return to Artenay, she decided that would be the safest and best option, especially since the aircrew escort wasn't due to take place until the following day.

Without delay Mabel navigated the shortest possible route to the railway station. The next train to Artenay was not for another 50 minutes, so she sat down on one of the station benches and used the time to observe those coming and going.

Some faces she recognised from previous visits to the station, so she could perhaps gather some useful intelligence for the cause.

*

It was early evening by the time Mabel found herself back in Artenay, a lengthy train delay contributing to this. She noticed the increasingly lush and verdant landscape with each passing week, although these glimpses of early summer were tempered somewhat by the increasing restrictions of life under the Germans.

The last lingering rays of the evening sun stroked Mabel's back as she reached the farmhouse. Surprisingly neither Di nor Alain were inside, a few unprepared vegetables lay on the kitchen table, but there was no evidence that an evening meal had been eaten. Mabel called out, but when it became obvious no one was present she decided to look outside. She felt her heartbeat accelerate slightly as she worried that Di and Alain had been arrested by the Germans. Walking around to the rear of the property, these fears were quickly allayed as Mabel could hear their voices. Immediately she let out an enormous sigh of relief that they were both safe, and followed the cacophony of noise; they were both obviously enjoying themselves.

The shrill laughter increased as Mabel approached the river. The sight of both Di and Alain naked and splashing around in the river stunned her. She immediately thought of Eddie, and knew that this wasn't right. Mabel took a few steps backwards before she was seen. Upset and not sure what to do, she then began to walk back to the farmhouse, before pausing and calling out for Di and Alain. She didn't want her sister to know that she had caught her being unfaithful to her husband. Eventually Di and Alain appeared, this time more modestly clothed. Mabel knew that this was an admission of guilt. However sick she felt at the thought of what had happened, Mabel had a job to do and needed to report back what had happened in Étampes.

She found it difficult to look her sister in the eye for any length of time, so she deliberately focused on repeating what had happened to Alain.

"You did brilliantly Mabel. Well done. It sounds very much like the Gestapo have their suspicions about Lucille. We will halt the movement of the aircrew tomorrow. Come on Di, we had better radio Paris and London."

Mabel was relieved that the two of them started to walk towards the farmhouse; she really didn't want to make small talk with her sister. After allowing them to get further ahead of her, Mabel started to follow up the path. She was still reeling from what had happened. So far Di had proved to be a good friend as well as a sister when she needed to talk through a problem. In this instance, though, she had no one to confide in. She dreaded sitting down for the evening meal later that night, so she grabbed some food and made the excuse that she was feeling exhausted from her long day. Part of her felt she should be there to monitor the conduct of the pair of them, but it was just too soon after what she had seen at the river. It made her sick with worry thinking about it. Later that night she lay awake in bed still thinking. Reflecting back, little signs had been there all along; the gentle touching, the rapport, laughing at each other's jokes and the longing gazes. Perhaps if she had noticed and acted earlier, this all could have been avoided.

Alain had already left the farmhouse when Mabel came down for breakfast the next morning. She was still unsure what to do; whether she should tackle her sister or let the matter lie. Fortunately, Di had details of her next assignment, which came as a much-desired distraction. The two aircrew who were due to be escorted down the line by Lucille today would now make the journey tomorrow. Mabel's task was to get back on the train and make her way to Étampes where she would observe and follow the new guide.

The journey from Artenay to Étampes had become commonplace for Mabel. She knew the countryside off by heart now, and was instantly able to pinpoint where she was on any one journey. She also knew all the nuances of the train service; which trains were most likely to be delayed, where the delays took place and even the most likely locations for checks by the Germans. Her papers had been checked many times now, and despite the death penalty awaiting her should her real identity be discovered, she found herself at ease playing the part of the 22-year-old Nadine Bertrand, fertiliser agent.

For the first time since arriving in France, some quite unpleasant weather descended upon the Artenay area. Thunderstorms and torrential downpours transformed the previously bright and idyllic landscape into a dark, almost menacing one. Fortunately, she had come prepared and packed suitable attire in her overnight bag.

On her arrival at Etampes railway station she had strict instructions to follow. Having found a vacant telephone kiosk, she carefully dialled the number of the farmhouse in Artenay. After a couple of rings Di's voice came onto the line.

"Hello."

"Could I speak to Henri Legrande please?" enquired Mabel.

"I'm sorry there is no one here with that name."

"I'm very sorry to have bothered you. Goodbye."

Mabel replaced the receiver, and checked her watch. She had 40 minutes to be in place outside the new guide's house. The new guide, Guylaine, lived in one of the larger properties on the outskirts of Étampes. Unlike Lucille, who shared her house with other females, Guylaine lived only with her father. In light of this, Alain felt it unnecessary to accompany Mabel to point her out. He had also provided her with a full description, and the best place to hide in order to watch the property.

Mabel reached the outer suburbs of Étampes some 20 minutes later. She hadn't hung around as the heavy rainfall continued with a relentless intensity. The outskirts of the town were devoid of much activity, not only because of the inclement weather but also due to the increasing number of properties being abandoned by those fleeing the Nazis. Within a few minutes Mabel had spotted the derelict house she was to use as her base to watch Guylaine. She was extremely thankful that her hiding place was undercover. It had now been raining for at least four hours and showed no sign of abating. She felt a little cold, and dearly wished for a cup of coffee. Hopefully, Guylaine, if she were the traitor, would either visit a contact or receive one very soon. Mabel took out some bread and cheese she had brought from the farmhouse and began to tuck in. Checking her wristwatch again, she knew instructions would be delivered to Guylaine in just under ten minutes. She peered across the road, through the gloom to the facing property. Set back from the road, the untidy grounds mirrored the general decay which had affected what was once an undoubtedly grand residence.

At precisely the agreed time, a young girl on a delivery bike cycled up to the property and carried a sack to the front door. Shortly the door opened and the sack was passed to another girl; Mabel assumed that the latter was Guylaine. She didn't get as good a view of her face as she had hoped since the heavy rain made that difficult. She wasn't unduly concerned though, since Guylaine was the only female living in the property so there was little risk of her tailing the wrong person.

Mabel waited patiently, staring through the incessant rain towards Guylaine's house. She had waited over two hours so far, and was beginning to wonder if Guylaine would leave at all. Perhaps the wet weather had delayed her making contact, although it had almost stopped raining now. The clearing skies enabled a sharper view of the house opposite. She considered creeping over to the property and having a discreet look round, but decided it would be far too risky during daylight hours. There was of course every chance that this house possessed a telephone, and perhaps Guylaine had made contact that way. The house had clearly once been one of Étampes's grander properties, and there were telephone lines entering it.

Mabel was just about to call it a day and seek out some accommodation for the night when the front door opened and the girl, wrapped in a knee-length raincoat and headscarf appeared. There were no other people about so Mabel would have to let Guylaine get quite a head start before she followed. It had started to rain again which actually pleased her since she would be able to wrap up well and conceal her face, and it would also make it more difficult for Guylaine to notice she was being followed.

Guylaine was a rapid walker, and Mabel became a little concerned that she may lose her if they entered the town centre where there were more people. They did appear to be heading that way. Fortunately, few shoppers had ventured out on such an unpleasant day, so it was easy for Mabel to spot Guylaine as she strode along the main street. It seemed increasingly likely that she was making her way to the station, but this was not the case as she walked beyond it and towards a part of the town Mabel was unfamiliar with. After a couple of blocks Guylaine entered Étampes hospital. Even before Mabel reached the hospital entrance, she knew she had, in all probability, lost Guylaine to the labyrinth of corridors. She couldn't very well roam the wards, so she had little choice but to retreat and think about her next step.

Mabel walked back to the main thoroughfare and found a window seat in a well-placed bar on the route Guylaine had taken. Her theory was that Guylaine would have to return sooner or later and would have to pass the station and the rows of bars and shops to reach home. The most likely explanation for Guylaine going to the hospital was surely to visit a sick relative or friend. She would have to check with Alain or Di on her return. If she was visiting, then it may be some time before she returned, Mabel reasoned. She therefore decided to order some food and settled for her usual dish of an omelette. Of course, she still had to find a room to stay in, but she couldn't foresee any problems on a quiet rainy night in

Étampes. After finishing her meal, Mabel ordered another coffee to extend her stay in the bar. She had been in France for nearly two months now, and had still not tasted one of the light-coloured beers that all the locals seemed to drink. She recollected the time her own father had allowed her to try one of the Simpson Breweries fine ales, not an experience she fondly remembered.

About an hour had elapsed since she had sat down in the bar, when Guylaine, huddled under her scarf and raincoat, walked hurriedly past the bar window. Mabel downed the last few mouthfuls of her already cold coffee, said farewell to the patron, and left. Guylaine's route was exactly the same as before, but in reverse. It became patently clear that she was returning home and wouldn't be meeting anyone. Having arrived at that conclusion, Mabel watched Guylaine disappear further along the road to her house, before turning back towards the town centre to seek out a hotel for the night.

Mabel was up early the next morning so that she could be in position in the derelict property opposite Guylaine's house. Apart from one or two moments of excitement, her assignments had largely been devoid of any drama, and today would probably be no different. Mabel was able to tail Guylaine at some distance since she knew she would be heading towards the railway station to escort the two aircrew. She followed all three to Tours without incident before returning to the farmhouse at Artenay.

*

"Wow," I remarked when Nan had finished, "so you actually followed an officer of the Gestapo. Wasn't that scary?"

"Not really," replied Nan modestly, "I didn't realise who he was at first, but he was only another human being. An evil one, yes, but still a human being."

"What if he had seen you?"

"I probably wouldn't be here now, and nor would you!" Nan replied calmly in a matter-of-fact manner, glossing over the gravity of the matter.

By now all of the stalls which constituted Baldock market had packed up and left, as the many café customers enjoyed the late afternoon sun. With a good effort, I would be able to get Nan back in time for afternoon tea.

"We'll have tea at one of the cafes another afternoon." I suggested.

"Agreed." Nan replied.

Back at the home, once Nan was settled with her cup of tea and pink wafer, I got up to leave.

"If it's a nice day, come again tomorrow, but come early as the next part of the story is quite long. Also, we need to go somewhere private."

I was quite intrigued by this, and would have to consider carefully where I should take her. Walking back to the car, my mind was formulating several possibilities as to which location would be best.

Chapter 6

The next day I visited Nan late in the morning. My plan was to take her on a walk with a picnic for lunch. Needless to say, I had packed a number of cheese-based items in my rucksack! A walk out into the countryside beyond Baldock's built-up environs would afford the privacy needed for what I hoped would be a long and interesting next instalment of Nan's life story.

Once we had left Templars, I pushed Nan's wheelchair in the direction of the Bogs. It undoubtedly sounds like the last place you would want to visit for a walk and a picnic. However, in the last 20 years the area has been transformed into an attractive wetland habitat. The town's rubbish dump which both Nan and I played on as children has since been covered with topsoil and landscaped with trees and plants which have gradually colonised and transformed the area. The river Ivel has been diverted so that it feeds a larger area of marshland, and various seats and picnic benches have been placed throughout. One or two areas remained untouched from Nan's childhood days; an old Anderson shelter and gunning post, both remnants of World War II.

With some difficulty I managed to push Nan in her wheelchair up the uneven path to the highest point of the

Bogs, or Ivel Springs as they are now called. The small grassy hill was in fact the largest of the rubbish tips, so we were in effect sitting on several decades of Baldock household waste. Our position gave us a prime view of the Bogs and the tallest buildings of Baldock, including St Mary's church poking out from behind the railway embankment which separated the town from the Bogs. After unpacking lunch, I waited patiently for Nan to continue her story.

1941

Mabel felt that with every assignment now, she was edging closer to the truth. The incident with the Gestapo officer appeared to be concrete evidence of this. Yet there was the possibility that he was unconnected to the escape line mole, but whatever the truth was, Mabel could sense that she was entering a particularly dangerous phase of her investigation. She thought of the many thousands of fellow countrymen and women who had already sacrificed their lives in the pursuit of the common good; she certainly had no intention of throwing in the towel any time soon.

Since returning from Étampes, Mabel had tried to avoid her sister. She felt able to speak with Alain more easily, despite the fact that he too was a guilty party. Mabel knew this, but couldn't help blaming her sister more. Di had always been the strong, level-headed member of the family and should have been able to resist, whatever the situation. Alain wasn't married, but Di was. Alain was able to find Mabel jobs on the farm, as well as one or two information-collecting assignments for the escape line.

Considering the incident with the Gestapo officer, and the increasing number of checks and searches being conducted,

Mabel and Alain decided to travel separately to Étampes for the next assignment, Mabel by train and Alain in his truck. This way the odds of both of them being apprehended were greatly reduced.

The train journey had transitioned from being a novelty to one of tedium. Prior to her time in France, she had only ridden by train on less than a handful of occasions. She now felt glad that she had never had to commute to work, and felt very sure, once the war was over, she wouldn't want to take another train trip in her life. She always felt like having a nap on the journey from Artenay to Étampes but knew that she had to be alert at all times.

The next guide she was to tail was known as Edith. Edith's family owned a small café on Étampes's main street, so it provided perfect cover for Alain to deliver his vegetables and produce. Like all French bars, omelettes were a speciality and fresh eggs from the farm at Artenay were included in the delivery. With a central location, Mabel was able to treat herself to the luxury of a hotel room as her base. Alain had made the reservation for the room which, probably not by chance, overlooked the main street and the café where Edith worked. She and her family lived in the flat above. Mabel was very grateful for the room. Firstly, it provided warmth and shelter, in contrast to the derelict shell she had used when watching Guylaine, and secondly, she could observe unnoticed from a distance instead of frequenting numerous bars and cafes for hours on end, which never sat entirely comfortably with her. As a young girl growing up in Baldock, pubs were the domain of men and it was not fitting for a young girl to enter one alone, although in truth the French equivalents were far less daunting.

After checking in, Mabel made her way to the main street below and located a bar almost opposite Edith's. Mabel positioned herself in a seat far enough away from the bar itself to avoid being distracted by any conversation that the patron might strike up. It was still a little early for workers to be having a drink on their way home from work, so the only customers were a few old timers chatting amongst themselves. Although Mabel thought it unlikely that they would engage in conversation with her, she took out one of the fake record books for the RACC that she always carried and pretended to study it. By the time her cheese omelette had arrived, the bar had started to fill up and she felt less conspicuous. Mabel had grown very partial to the hard French cheeses used in the omelettes and had even started to experiment by purchasing different varieties in the delicatessens on her travels. The soft cheeses had yet to win her over; the strong aromas being the biggest barrier to gaining her favour.

Right on cue, Alain arrived at the agreed time, and shifted a crate of assorted produce from the back of his truck and into Edith's café. A young woman with long flowing brown hair followed him back outside to the rear of the truck where he handed her some trays of eggs. After a brief exchange, Alain was back inside the cab driving off to make the next delivery. With Edith identified, Mabel finished the rest of her omelette, keeping one eye on the café opposite. She assumed that it was very unlikely that Edith would leave the café anytime soon since there were now a lot more people on the street and she would be kept busy serving customers for the next couple of hours or so. With the hotel room nearby, Mabel had no need to prolong her stay in the bar, so she paid the bill and left.

Back in the hotel room Mabel positioned the room's one chair so that she could observe Edith's café, but far enough away from the window so that she couldn't be seen from the outside. This was absolutely the worst part of the job, waiting hours on end for something to happen. Mabel found that she had to keep getting up from the chair and walking around the room every so often to ease some of the boredom and to stop herself from nodding off. A steady flow of customers continued to enter and leave the café until curfew arrived. Once the last customer had left, Mabel watched Edith and other members of her family, most likely her mother and father, clean and prepare the café for the morning. With the café shut for the night, this would be the time most likely for Edith to make any move to make contact if she was the mole, although being on the main street of Étampes surely made that almost impossible during curfew. Making contact in the morning would be much easier.

In the room above the café Mabel could now see Edith, her parents and a younger child entering the room and taking seats, no doubt relaxing after a hard day's work. After about half an hour when the night had closed in further, Edith drew the curtains. Mabel predicted that there would almost certainly be nothing more to observe this evening, and once she was fairly satisfied this was the case, she retired to bed for the night.

Mabel rose early the next morning, as her usual syndrome of not being able to sleep well in a strange bed had prevented any lengthy dormancy. She wasn't too bothered since she needed to be up early to follow Edith down the escape line. Mabel had expected her to make the five-minute walk to the station at about a quarter past eight in time for the half past the hour service to Tours. It was then a huge shock when she opened the curtains at just after seven o'clock to witness Edith leave the café and walk hurriedly and purposefully along the main street towards the station. Mabel was in a quandary; she could either observe Edith from the hotel window for a short time, or quickly rush downstairs and attempt to follow her knowing full well that she could be out of sight by the time she reached street level.

Realistically she knew that there was only one option, and that was to make an attempt to follow her; watching from the hotel room would yield nothing. This was perhaps just the lead that she had been waiting for. Hurtling down the stairs, and fortunately meeting no other guests on the way, Mabel soon found herself on the main street. She knew that it would be unwise to start running in an effort to make up lost ground, so she walked as briskly as she could in the direction of the railway station scanning both the street ahead and the insides of any bars or shops that were open at this early hour. It became increasingly apparent with every passing minute that Edith had probably entered one of these premises and had disappeared from view.

Mabel had now reached the railway station. She glanced inside and surveyed the booking hall. Edith was using the telephone. Mabel moved towards the tobacco kiosk situated a few feet away from the telephone in order to attempt to hear what was being said. However just as she got to within hearing distance, Edith replaced the receiver and started to walk out of the building. Mabel now had a big decision to make. Should she call Di and issue instructions to abort the movement of the aircrew down the escape line, or allow it to go ahead? She wasn't in possession of any hard evidence that the mission had been compromised, but she had also been taught to err on the side of caution. It was now twenty minutes past seven, so she had just over an hour before Edith would pick up the aircrew. She quickly decided to follow Edith who retraced her steps back to the café. Mabel continued, walked past the café and crossed the street to the same bar she had dined in on the previous evening. She didn't want to make a rash decision so she ordered a coffee and croissant while she mulled over her options.

Mabel racked her brains in order to explain why Edith had gone to the station to make a call an hour before she was due to make her way to the station anyway. Was it so that the Germans could be ready at Étampes station to arrest the aircrew? It just seemed very clumsy and unlikely, and almost certain to lead to suspicions being raised against Edith. If Edith had contacted the Germans in order for the aircrew to be arrested at Étampes, then it was certainly too late for Mabel to do anything about it. The aircrew would already be en route from Paris. She would just have to tail the group and hope for the best. Mabel paid her bar bill and left to walk back along the main street to the station. By now the street was thronging with townspeople going about their business. She intended to be in position before Edith returned to accompany the aircrew. Strangely Edith's café appeared to be shut, leading Mabel to question her own powers of observation. Had it been closed earlier and had she not noticed? Either way she began to feel uneasy. She was tempted to cross the road and investigate further, but she didn't want to run the risk of bumping into Edith as she left for the station, and time was now pressing.

The station was now extremely congested, in contrast to the relative quiet of an hour before. Mabel managed to squeeze onto the end of one of the station benches and took out her trusty RACC record book, making out she was checking some details. At twenty-five minutes past eight Edith had still not arrived at the station which worried Mabel greatly that a raid was about to take place. However, looking around, it was apparent that there were no more Germans present than normal, so perhaps everything was going to work out fine. Two minutes later the locomotive forming the 8.30 service to Tours puffed its way into the station. Just at this moment, Valeria, the very first guide Mabel had tailed, walked towards the platform where the advancing train was slowly coming to a halt. Realising that she would now be following Valeria again, Mabel quickly took out a pair of glasses from her bag and put them on. Fortunately, she had also dyed her hair since that first conversation with her, so her appearance was quite different now, and the risk of being recognised reduced.

Mabel's brain continued to compute all the possible reasons for the change of guide and concluded that the most likely explanation was some emergency had prompted Edith to cancel, and Valeria was a last-minute replacement. Hence the café was shut, and for this reason Valeria had arrived so late. Satisfied that everything seemed alright, Mabel decided against making a coded phone call to Di to abort the mission, and started to make her way over to the platform. This time, to be on the safe side, Mabel chose a different carriage to the one that Valeria entered.

Being rush hour, all of the carriages and compartments were filling up to capacity with only a few seats available. Mabel found a one next to the corridor so that she could exit quickly should the need arise. She once again removed her trusty RACC record book from her bag and began to settle down for the long journey to Tours, hoping that it would turn out to be worthwhile. Although she didn't feel that Valeria was the mole, it was on one of her journeys that the train had been stopped and searched. Without Mabel's quick thinking, aircrew would have almost certainly been captured. She began to consider the operation from the mole's point of view. In order to allay any suspicions from the escape line, the informer was unlikely to tip off the Germans about one's own run. Theories of double-bluff entered Mabel's mind, which she quickly dismissed to stop herself being inundated with too many conflicting and ridiculous ideas. Apart from Alain, Di, London, Paris and the guide for each individual trip, no one else would be aware. Étampes did seem to be a recurring theme though. To take her mind off these theories of double-bluff, Mabel stared out of the window and admired the leafy and virescent tranquillity of the French countryside. At times it was very difficult to comprehend that a world war was taking place. She was certainly more fortunate than most. The spies working in the north of the country and in the Paris, region had the added danger of air raids which she had learnt had hit a number of trains in those areas with many casualties. At least the planes rarely ventured this far south.

The train had just passed through Artenay, which left Chevilly, Fluery les Aubrais and Orléans before the second leg of the journey to Tours. Mabel wondered what Alain and Di would get up to later that day once he had returned from making deliveries. Trying not to dwell on this unsavoury topic for too long, Mabel started to think about her parents and how proud they would be of her and her sister's efforts to shorten the war.

As the train pulled into Fluery les Aubrais station, a businessman who was sitting next to the window in Mabel's compartment let out a groan and uttered a comment about there being more delays. Mabel looked up from the record book to see that German troops lined the platform. As the train eased to a halt, it did cross her mind that this was the same station that the train was searched on her very first assignment. Valeria was the guide that day too. The predictable fierce and loud-mouthed German in charge barked out the usual instructions for everyone to vacate the train. Shuffling along the crowded corridor Mabel glanced out of the window and onto the platform below to see if Valeria and the aircrew were down there yet. Initially there was no sign of them, but as Mabel clambered down the steps from the carriage, she spotted two possible aircrew descending the steps on the adjacent carriage. Once Mabel had joined the line of frustrated and in many cases, scared passengers on the platform, she could see Valeria ahead of her, probably about six people or so behind what she thought were the aircrew. Mabel wondered if it was significant, they were being searched at the same place as before, or was it simply the rigid and efficient German way of carrying out such procedures.

At the head of the queue a couple of German soldiers were searching any bags and luggage that passengers presented. Alongside them was the loud-mouthed officer who had ordered everyone off the train, and with him another man dressed in civvies. Mabel was unsure what his role was, but whatever it was, he was doing virtually all of the talking to the passengers. It was only when she drew closer that she realised that he was a native French speaker. Her initial thought and understandable worry were that he would expose her as an outsider. Quickly though she began to appreciate that the two aircrew, assuming that her guess was accurate, were in grave danger. However, there was nothing she could do, except stand patiently in line and let events unfold. Now in earshot of the questioning, Mabel understood the interpreter was using a variety of phrases and words which would render a basic grasp of the language redundant.

The two aircrew were now at the head of the queue and placed their small tatty tan-coloured suitcases onto the tables which had been hauled out from inside the station buildings. The French inquisitor started to question one of the men, when the other one pushed past the makeshift barrier and started to sprint towards the end of the platform. After a few shouted orders of 'halt', a round of machine guns sprayed bullets into the back of the escaping airman leaving him spread-eagled and face-down on the grey concrete platform. The other airman, visibly shocked, turned around and looked at Valeria for some guidance. Valeria dropped her head immediately, but it was too late.

"You there," the German Officer pointed at Valeria. She kept her head lowered, but the officer stepped forward and shouted out another order.

"Arrest that girl."

Two German soldiers started to move towards her when she threw her bag into one of their faces, turned around and threw herself under the stationery train and onto the tracks.

"After her," The officer bawled.

At least a dozen soldiers joined the chase which quickly ended when a salvo of machine-gun fire rang out, echoing in and around the station buildings. One of the soldiers re-joined the officer to convey the news that the girl had been shot and was dead.

"Everyone back on the train," the officer yelled.

Mabel joined the throng of other passengers eager to escape the brutality of the Nazis, by quickly mounting the steps of the carriage. Back in the compartment, she advanced to the window in dreaded anticipation of viewing Valeria's corpse. Her lifeless body lay face-up with a pool of blood, trickling away from her towards the station building. Mabel regarded her face; the look of absolute terror would stay with her for the rest of her life. She felt as though she was about to cry, but somehow managed to pull herself together as the other passengers re-joined her in the compartment. She could sense some gasps of horror, but also the fact that such commonplace brutal events had enabled some citizens to build up resistance to appalling happenings.

Mabel was disgusted though, watching as Valeria's body was unceremoniously picked up and carried away by two German soldiers. Moments later the locomotive started to slowly pick up speed and haul itself out of the station passing the pool of blood, telling evidence of such a violent death. She would now abort her journey to Tours and leave the train at the next station, Orléans, and return to Artenay.

The next train back up the line to Artenay was not due for another 50 minutes, so Mabel decided to wander into Orléans. Her father had always said that a good stiff drink was the best remedy for shock. Mabel had seldom touched alcohol; for one thing she didn't like the taste and also, growing up in a small traditional market town, pubs were not the place for young ladies to frequent. She quickly decided against ordering any alcohol and instead found a respectable looking café where she ordered a coffee to soothe her frayed nerves. After a few gulps, Mabel began to feel a little less shaky, and attempted to process the events of the morning. It dawned on her that the Germans were definitely tipped off that aircrew were on the train. Why else would everyone else be waved back onto the train once the aircrew had been caught? It was a targeted attack, but who was responsible? It certainly wasn't Valeria. She had been extremely brave and sacrificed her life, and by doing so had protected the rest of the escape line. She would have known that, had she been captured, she would have been tortured by the Gestapo for what little information she possessed, and therefore had attempted her suicidal escape.

The Nazis really were incredibly stupid, thought Mabel. They always seemed to shoot first and ask questions later; in this case none were possible because the guide had been killed and, with false papers on her, the trail would also stop dead almost immediately. The one airman that had been detained had only met her a few hours previously and would have no information to shed on the mechanics of the escape line. With Valeria dead, was Edith the culprit? It seemed implausible and too obvious. Perhaps it had more to do with Lucille being followed by the Gestapo officer, and possibly they had discovered Étampes station was a transfer point and observed Valeria at the station earlier that morning. Why then had Alain used her? Mabel started to formulate a long list of questions she wanted to ask him and Di when she returned to the farmhouse.

Leaving the train at Artenay, Mabel just wanted to get back to the farmhouse as quickly as possible. The horrific and brutal nature of the killings was now beginning to sink in, and she badly needed the attention of a loved one in order to bring some normality back to her life. She hadn't felt that close to her sister recently, but she now desperately wanted to be with her. No amount of training could have prepared her for the events at Fluery les Aubrais that morning. Since she had returned early it was only mid-afternoon, and as she had hoped, Alain was elsewhere on the farm which meant that she could spend some time with Di alone. Word had obviously not got back to her sister yet, who was genuinely surprised to see her. Mabel started to cry as she advanced towards her sister.

"What is it, Mabel?" Di asked, putting down the wicker basket she had been carrying.

"It was horrible," Mabel fell into the arms of her sister and sobbed. Di allowed her sister to give in to her emotions before taking her inside where she poured out a measure of brandy.

"Mabel, I know you don't drink, but have this. It will help."

Mabel took the tumbler and swigged down a mouthful of the spirit, grimacing as she did so. After taking another mouthful, Di offered her sister a handkerchief, which she took and started to wipe her face and eyes dry.

"Take your time, and tell me what happened."

Mabel started to recount all that had happened that day beginning with the unexpected change of guide, which Di acknowledged that Alain and herself knew about. She then proceeded to give details of what happened at Fluery les Aubrais – which became increasingly difficult as the narration progressed.

When Mabel had finished, Di spoke.

"I'm so sorry. We should have never sent Valeria, but she was the only one we could get to stand in at the last moment.

We should have waited and checked things out more thoroughly."

"What happened to Edith?" Mabel enquired, placing the empty glass onto the table. The effect of the brandy had eased her nerves significantly.

"Her mother was taken ill in the middle of the night, and by the time she contacted us the aircrew were already being sent down from Paris. We thought it would be alright using Valeria, but obviously it wasn't. That poor girl."

Mabel wiped her eyes once more with the handkerchief. "So do you think Edith had anything to do with it?"

"It seems a little too convenient. I will check out her story and ask Alain when he gets in. He knows all the guides and their families. He will have a good idea."

Dinner that evening was a sombre affair. All three of them were in shock at losing one of their own as well as an airman. Di had managed to confirm with one of her agents at Étampes hospital that Edith's mother had been admitted in the early hours of the morning with severe stomach pains. The diagnosis was ongoing. Alain vouched for Edith and her family.

Alain addressed Mabel. "You don't ever get over it. You just learn to live with it. It will get easier in time."

Mabel nodded, before Alain continued.

"If you do decide this line of work is not for you, and want to return to England, we will both understand and respect your decision."

Mabel nodded again before replying, "No, it's been a shock, but I'm even more determined than ever to carry on and get to the bottom of this."

"Good girl Mabel," Alain placed his hands on top of Mabel's and gave her a reassuring smile.

*

Her next mission down the escape line was in a few days, and on this occasion one of the three aircrew to be returned was deemed to be of significant importance to the war effort.

"I'm not sure we should let her know how important he is."

Di, Alain and Mabel sat around the kitchen table discussing the forthcoming transportation of the three aircrew. Di had raised the point that one airman really was of high importance and, by telling the guide that, they could be presenting the information on a plate for the enemy.

"I think it's a risk worth taking if Mabel can expose the traitor, and there will always be a chance that she can alert us and we can abort," Alain countered.

After a couple more exchanges, Di reluctantly agreed that the guide, Marie, would be informed.

"Mabel, I want you to take this with you," Alain produced a small handgun from underneath the table.

"It's just a precaution, you never know. You did tail that Gestapo man last week, and I feel you must be getting close to stumbling upon something. Keep it concealed on your body, and never keep it in any of your bags."

Di placed a hand on Mabel's as she reached out and took the gun.

"Be careful Mabel."

"I will," she replied, touched at her sister's response, and decided she must spend some time with her before leaving on this next mission. The plan was exactly the same as last time, to be in position when Marie received notification and then track her movements before following her down the line.

In the 24 hours leading up to Marie taking the three aircrew down the line, Mabel tailed her movements in Étampes without discovering any unusual actions. She had firstly gone shopping in the morning and then completed her waitressing job in the evening. Mabel chose to have her evening meal at the bar where Marie worked. To reduce the risk of her being recognised the following day, Mabel had radically altered her appearance by changing her clothes and wearing a wig and some glasses.

When Mabel retired to bed later that night, she was fairly satisfied that Marie had acted normally throughout the day and had witnessed no evidence to suggest that she was the traitor. Tomorrow looked like being another routine day.

The following morning, heavy rain once again greeted Mabel as she drew back the curtains. With her disguise from the previous evening discarded, Mabel resumed her normal appearance, although her raincoat and scarf effectively enabled a third change in 24 hours. Despite the wet weather, Marie adopted a casual stroll to the station. En route she did not stop to speak to anyone, and made her way directly to the station. Mabel had worked out which train service to Tours she would be catching, so she tailed her at some distance to ensure she was not detected. The station seemed slightly busier than normal; perhaps there had been some delays and the number of passengers waiting had swelled. From Mabel's position, close to the entrance, she saw Marie standing on platform two holding a magazine. She gave the appearance of just another passenger bored with waiting for her train. Mabel was scanning the station for any suspicious figures or behaviour when her eyes fell upon Guylaine, the girl she had followed down the line the previous week. Dressed in the same raincoat and scarf, she sat on one of the station seats probably observing the scene just as she herself was doing.

As the train chugged into the station Mabel watched Guylaine make her way to platform two where she stopped and waited about ten feet from Marie. Mabel felt a little uneasy, or was it just a coincidence that two guides were waiting to board the same train. She also started to walk over to the platform as a number of the passengers alighted. Ahead of her, both Marie and Guylaine climbed on board the same carriage. Mabel was just about to follow suit when she noticed Guylaine exit the door at the opposite end of the same carriage. Her gut instinct, not for the first time, had proved correct; something wasn't quite right. Mabel stopped herself from entering the carriage and pretended to be waving someone off as Guylaine walked past her. Maintaining her position, with one eye on Guylaine, she followed her movements. She had walked over to the telephone kiosk and was now making a call.

Mabel's uneasiness increased as she began to feel real danger for the aircrew. Was Guylaine telephoning the authorities? Alain and Di hadn't mentioned anything about her being involved today. It was necessary to act fast and take decisive action. Mabel decided not to board the train and instead waited for Guylaine to leave the station, before walking over to the phone herself. Before she could get there, a middle-aged woman had picked up the receiver and was now making a call. Seemingly in no hurry, the woman appeared to be chatting about nothing in particular, as Mabel started to tap her foot impatiently. She tried to catch the woman's eye to convey that she needed to use the phone immediately. Mabel knew she didn't have much time. Staying as calm as she could, she waited for the phone to become free again. She just hoped that someone at the farmhouse was there to take her call. Shortly Di answered the phone and Mabel gave the coded message to abort. She just hoped that the resistance could stop the train in time and get the aircrew off.

The next train southbound departed nearly 30 minutes late. For Mabel this was one of the most interminably long journeys she had ever taken. She just wanted to be back at the farmhouse to find out if her warning had been successful in allowing time for the aircrew to be safely taken off the train.

Three stops further down the line from Étampes, the train was halted at Toury and all passengers ordered off; the Germans were checking all the luggage and paperwork of every person aboard the train. If this search was related to the aircrew, then it was possibly a good omen. They were still looking and therefore they must have escaped, before the previous train service was stopped and searched. Mabel still had the small handgun on her person, but her good sense meant she had disposed of the wig she had used in Étampes. As long as her papers were in order and the contents of her case aroused no suspicion, she felt reasonably confident she would be allowed to pass through without any thorough body search. Mabel always assumed one day she may be questioned further and possibly taken into custody. The checks seemed to be taking longer than usual, as if the Germans weren't entirely sure what they were looking for, and therefore conducting very thorough examinations.

Mabel felt a little uneasy, but having almost certainly unmasked the traitor, she wasn't going to be caught without following through her mission to a satisfactory end. When it was her turn, the guard asked a couple more questions than usual, but these appeared to be fairly standard and not especially troubling for her to answer. If the Germans were still looking for a young French girl with three aircrew, then they would not be in luck.

Eventually, after a long and fruitless search, the train was in motion again. With no further hold-ups, Mabel soon found herself in Artenay, walking along the lane to the farmhouse. She considered how she might warn Di and Alain she was coming; after all she dreaded repeating the awful position that she had found herself in the previous week. Before she reached the door to the farmhouse, she called out both their names. When she entered the kitchen, much to Mabel's relief, they were both seated at the kitchen table.

"Well, are they safe?" Mabel had only just closed the door behind her when she fired the question at the two of them.

"They are thanks to you. Excellent work, Mabel." replied Alain. "We took them off at Toury and had them holed up in a safe house."

Mabel described to them the search at Toury earlier. It was her sister who then spoke.

"That sounds bad. They might be conducting house-to-house searches. I'll radio later to find out what's going on."

"So, what happened in Étampes for you to call for an abort?" asked Alain.

Mabel described what happened at the railway station, and in conclusion asked, "so it looks like Guylaine is our mole then?"

"On the face of it, yes. It looks as if she waits at the station to see if there are any possible aircrew and then passes the information on to the Germans. This might explain why the captures have been so sporadic; else the Germans would be bound to smash the whole line."

"Unless of course they are being clever?" suggested Di.

"I can't believe it of Guylaine though," continued Alain, "she's always been one of our best operatives. A true patriot. She hates the Germans. Di, radio London and Paris and see what they can find out. Mabel, in the meantime, make the journey back to Étampes and see what you can find out. Tail her, and we just might get the proof we need to be certain."

"Take the gun with you Mabel," interrupted Di.

"Yes," continued Alain, "and use it if you have to. Ring every evening just before curfew from the railway station, as near to 7 o'clock as you can make it. We'll agree to some codes to keep you updated."

Mabel was happy that Alain suggested that she go back to Étampes, not because she wanted to avoid him and Di, but to successfully complete her mission. She would have found it so frustrating if she had been pulled from the assignment before a clear and decisive conclusion had been reached.

Mabel spent much of the next morning travelling to Étampes on an increasingly erratic train service. Numerous hold-ups had prolonged her journey so that it was in fact lunchtime when she arrived. Mabel had brought some food with her, so she hurried towards the derelict hideout opposite where Guylaine lived. She had walked halfway up the road when a figure from the vicinity of Guylaine's house started walking towards her. Without a second glance, Mabel ascertained that it was Guylaine, and that she needed to avoid being seen close-up. Entering the grounds of the nearest house, which bore some resemblance to being agriculturally-related, Mabel knocked on the front door. Ideally, she wanted someone to be at home so that she could engage in conversation long enough for Guylaine to walk past, but equally she didn't want to be trapped in a lengthy dialogue about fertilisers which would cause her to lose sight of Guylaine. Fortunately, the woman who answered the door didn't require any fertilisers but exchanged a few pleasantries with Mabel before bidding her goodbye.

Mabel turned around to see that Guylaine, still dressed in a raincoat and scarf despite the absence of any precipitation, had passed her and was now advancing towards the town centre. Mabel dawdled between the front door and the street to allow Guylaine to establish a sizeable distance between the two of them.

Guylaine passed the station, as Mabel realised a little too late the young woman was heading towards the hospital again, and it would be impossible to close the gap sufficiently to be able to continue tailing her in the hospital. Mabel didn't even know Guylaine's surname so she couldn't ask at reception. She was curious to find out who she was visiting, but also appreciated it was highly unlikely her contact worked at, or was a patient of, the hospital. Her gut instinct told her that Guylaine was simply visiting either a relative or friend. If Guylaine visited the hospital most days, apart from those when she was taking aircrew down the escape line, then Mabel could find out who she was visiting another day. In the meantime, she would take the opportunity to have some food, assuming that Guylaine's visit would be of a similar length to that of the previous occasion. This way, Mabel could save the food she had bought with her and eat it when she was observing Guylaine from the derelict property later.

It was some time before Guylaine walked past the bar where Mabel had enjoyed a particularly satisfying cheese and mushroom omelette. She observed the guide walk in the direction of home. Mabel decided she would let her get a substantial distance ahead, to totally allay any lingering suspicions she might have that she was being followed. Although it hadn't rained today, it was rather chilly for the time of year, so Mabel was glad of the shelter from the north-westerly winds that gusted through the narrow streets of Étampes.

The subsequent hours passed very slowly. There were no visitors to the house and Guylaine made no more visits to the hospital or elsewhere. Mabel had decided that once it was dark, she would enter the grounds of Guylaine's house and begin to hunt around. She hadn't heard or seen any dogs, so she felt reasonably confident she would be able to do this undetected.

Before doing so, she first had to quickly venture into town to the railway station to phone Di. If she hurried it wouldn't take more than 30 minutes. It was just before twenty to seven when she started to dial the number of the farmhouse. Strangely there was no answer, so Mabel replaced the handset and carefully redialled the number. The ringing tone continued as the call remained unanswered. In the meantime, an impatient-looking businessman was now waiting to us the phone. Mabel replaced the receiver and checked her watch, 15 minutes to seven. She vacated the phone kiosk and began to walk back to the hideout, somewhat worried that something had gone wrong. There was always the chance the Germans would discover them one day, but was she being too pessimistic? Alain and Di were very skilled in covering their tracks. Or perhaps Guylaine had given them away? This was unlikely, since she knew nothing of Di's existence and none of the guides knew where Alain live. It seemed more likely that there had been an emergency on the farm, or they had simply forgotten that Mabel was due to phone and were elsewhere.

As night fell, an eerie darkness descended upon the area. Mabel though, was quite happy that there was no moonlight which made the possibility of detection much less likely. Furthermore, she had a detailed mental map of the house design and layout of the grounds. Dressed entirely in black, Mabel noiselessly crossed the street and started to advance towards the house, dodging a number of obstacles she had identified earlier in daylight.

She had reached the front of the house when a car's engine and headlights could be heard and seen advancing up the road from the town centre. Mabel ducked down to allow the car to pass by, only it began to slow and eventually stopped outside the property. Mabel, her adrenalin starting to increase, crawled on all fours to the side of the property to avoid being discovered. A light from inside the house partially illuminated some of the garden as the front door was opened and the visitor admitted. Once the door was closed, Mabel was left in almost complete darkness, but for a narrow shaft of light from a small window further along the side wall.

Mabel crept along the side of the property as quickly as she could, balancing the need to find out what was happening with the knowledge she was in an unfamiliar and dark territory in which she could easily stumble into something and give herself away. The window which was producing the shaft of light was too high up for her to look into, although she could make out some faint voices. Mabel advanced to the end of the side wall and glanced around the corner. The area was fairly well illuminated from the larger windows at the back of the property. It would be too risky to look into the room. Mabel had no choice but to stick with the side window, and to find a way of looking inside. With no ladder or other suitable equipment to hand, Mabel shimmied up a drainpipe onto the roof at the front of the property. She then carefully clambered across the roof to a ledge just above the side window, and gently lowered her head down into the window aperture.

Guylaine stood with her back to Mabel, her long brown hair at last exposed from beneath her headscarf. Facing her stood the man that had followed Lucille, the one Mabel had tailed back to the town hall. In all probability, Mabel was less than six feet away from a highly dangerous Gestapo agent. She strained to hear the conversation taking place.

"What…information do you……" asked the man.

Guylaine's response was inaudible.

"You know………if you don't," replied the man.

The precarious position Mabel found herself in was becoming increasingly uncomfortable, and placed significant strain on her tiring muscles. Seeking to readjust her position, one of the roof tiles slid from its position and crashed onto the ground. Mabel immediately realised she was in dire trouble as the Gestapo agent reacted to this noisy interruption, drew a gun from his pocket and started to move towards the back door. Mabel swung her body round and jumped off the ledge onto the soft ground below, before rolling behind a shrub. She could now hear the Gestapo man advance from the rear of the property.

"Show yourself immediately," the man ordered.

Mabel knew she had to act decisively. If she pretended, she wasn't there, then in all likelihood the man would have the area surrounded and searched until she was found. She only had one chance. In the dimness of the night, Mabel aimed the pistol at the man and shot him. The man slumped and fell to the ground. Beyond the wall, a second figure stood. Not Guylaine, but Brigitte Duval. Guylaine was a code name for Brigitte.

*

Nan broke off from her narrative, tears started to roll down her cheeks. She used her handkerchief to dab them away.

"So, what did you do?" I asked.

"I shot her."

I was stunned, and felt a numbness overcome me. It was Nan who spoke next.

"Take me back. I can't tell you anymore today, but come and see me tomorrow. I will tell you the rest of the story then."

I pushed Nan back to Templars in silence. While it had been fascinating to hear of Nan's wartime experiences, part of me felt as if I had exhumed a host of unpleasant memories for her. For that I felt upset at disturbing the past. When we reached the retirement home, Nan wanted to go to her room. For that I was grateful, I don't think either of us wanted to bump into Mrs Caunter and be questioned about any missing items.

"Are you going to be alright?" I asked her.

"Yes, I'm fine. You don't get to my age without some upset." Nan smiled at me, "See you tomorrow at the same time."

On leaving Nan, I couldn't help but admire what a remarkable woman she was, and still is.

Chapter 7

It was with some trepidation that I approached Templars the next day. I wasn't sure in what kind of mood I would find Nan, and perhaps she wouldn't want to carry on with her narrative. I needn't have worried though as she was in bright spirits, and evidently intent on causing some mischief. It was probably what we both needed after yesterday. As if on cue, Mrs Caunter started to advance down the corridor towards us. I groaned inwardly, dreading to think what Nan had done, or what she might say.

"Hello there, off out, are we?" she called down the corridor to us.

"No, we're just going to bed," Nan replied sarcastically.

Fortunately, the sarcasm seemed to go over Mrs Caunter's head, as I exchanged pleasantries with her before leaving.

The newly renovated memorial garden in Baldock Park was where I decided to take Nan today. I knew I had to find somewhere peaceful and private for Nan to continue with her story. It was unlikely that there would be any other visitors, and if there were we could find a quiet, secluded corner. Nan had always loved having flowers around the house, so I hoped the rich carpet of reds, blues, yellows, oranges and purples of the memorial garden would help her tell me what was probably going to be the most heart-wrenching part of her story.

1941

Brigitte's body slumped to the floor. Mabel knew that she had no choice but to shoot her. Had she let her go, Brigitte would have almost certainly contacted the Germans and Mabel would have been captured, tortured and killed.

Mabel bent down to check the pulse of the Gestapo agent. He was definitely dead. She repeated her actions on Brigitte's body, and discovered that she was still breathing. She had no idea where she had hit her or how life-threatening her injury was. Mabel shed a tear as she looked down upon the dimly-lit face of her childhood friend. She wanted to get help, but that would mean endangering the lives of the rest of the escape line volunteers, as well as her own.

Mabel knew that she had to leave the area as quickly as possible, but her options were virtually non-existent. No trains would be running at this late hour, so she thought about phoning Alain. She had found a telephone in Brigitte's house but she knew it would be bugged, and the night-time curfew made it impossible to return to the train station to use the phone there. She could lie low until the morning and make her way home then, but the Gestapo agent would probably have been missed by then and a search party sent out to investigate. Mabel realised that her chances of getting out of this were not great.

She walked back outside to where the bodies were, thinking that she should perhaps conceal them. It could potentially allow her more time to escape. Suddenly Mabel jumped out of her skin, when a man's voice called out her name in a loud whisper,

"Mabel, are you alone?"

"Yes," she replied, unsure if the voice was a friend or foe.

"It's me, Alain." From one of the bushes, her 'cousin' stepped out. "What happened?"

As calmly as she could, Mabel related the events of that evening. Alain leant over and checked the bodies.

"We need to get out of here now. My truck is parked up the road."

Mabel started to follow Alain.

"Wait, I need to get the gun."

"Hurry up."

In fact, Mabel had already secreted the gun on her person. When she re-entered the house Mabel picked up the telephone receiver and dialled the number of the hospital. She wanted to save the life of her friend, but also realised it may endanger the lives of all of those involved in the escape line. With this in mind she replaced the handset before leaving any details.

Mabel knew the danger was not over yet and that they were both out after curfew. For this reason, Alain stuck to the backroads.

"So how come you are here?" Mabel enquired, once she had got her head around the evening's events and began to think more lucidly.

"We'll talk about it back at the farmhouse. At the moment there is probably too much going on in your head to make sense of it all. Try to get some sleep. If we are stopped, the truck broke down earlier when we were making deliveries."

There was no chance of her falling asleep anytime soon, but Mabel knew there was no point in trying to prise any information out of Alain, so frustratingly she would just have to wait.

The cross-country route from Étampes to Artenay in the dark took considerably longer than the main roads or by train. Despite reaching the farmhouse at a very late hour, Di was still up to greet them.

"Thank God you're safe Mabel. I'm so sorry." Di warmly embraced her sister.

"Why should you be sorry?" Mabel glanced from Di to Alain, who was trying to shake his head in a discreet manner.

"What aren't you telling me?"

"Not now, in the morning."

Mabel for the first time persisted against Alain's wishes, "No, Di tell me now."

"Sorry for missing your call and not warning you."

"What was the message you were supposed to give me?"

"To abort and come back immediately."

"But I've probably just killed two people."

"What?"

Mabel relayed the evening's events to her visibly shocked sister.

"Oh my God. London's instructions were to leave Guylaine untouched. What have we done?

Alain interrupted, trying to be a voice of reason, "Look we don't know the full story. It was them or Mabel tonight. Which would you prefer?"

Di appeared to understand Alain's point, when Mabel spoke.

"So where were you when I phoned?"

Di looked at Alain, and hesitated. Suddenly Mabel twigged.

"You were with him, weren't you?"

Mabel looked from Di to Alain, but neither chose to reply.

"You were then? I killed two people tonight because you wanted a few more minutes with your fancy man. I shall never forgive you for this."

Mabel started to leave the room.

"Mabel..." Di started to speak.

"No, don't follow me. I mean it." Mabel spoke in an angry and determined manner which her sister had never witnessed before.

It would be many years before the two sisters spoke again.

*

Nan broke off from her narrative, and regarded me with one of her rueful looks.

"So that was my war," she stated as a matter of fact.

"But what happened next? Did you come home?"

"Yes, it was agreed in the circumstances that I should come back to England. I couldn't stay with Di, so I was sent down the line a short time later. I still worked for the service, training recruits. I know they were keen for me to go back behind enemy lines, but I couldn't go through all that again."

"So, did they debrief you and tell you why Brigitte was to be left untouched? Did you ever find out what happened to her?"

"I was debriefed, but on their terms. You're only told what you need to know. To this day I've never found out why those instructions were issued. They told me she went missing, so I've no idea what happened to her. I don't even know if she lived or died."

146

I could sense that even some 70 years later the mystery of what happened to Brigitte still haunted Nan. There was probably not much more she could tell me so I decided to move on.

"And after the war, you quietly slipped back into civilian life, and nobody was any the wiser?"

"Indeed, I did. My parents never found out. I wasn't allowed to tell them, the Official Secrets Act etc. I remember when my mother was in hospital following her fall, just before she died, I almost told her then."

Nan's mother, my great-grandmother, had died in 1972 at the age of 95, following a fall in which she broke her hip. I can just about remember her.

"But it would have been too much for her to take in. I often wish I had told her and my father before he died. I think it would have made them very proud."

"It would have done," I replied, "but you're telling me now, and I'm very proud of you. I know the rest of the family would be absolutely thrilled to hear your story."

"Possibly," Nan answered, "but not just yet. Promise me you won't say anything?"

"Very well. So, what did you do when the war was over?"

"Initially I went back to the FFHC, or Kayser Bondor as it became, but only very briefly. I became pregnant soon afterwards and left to become a full-time mother. Herbie, your grandfather, was a wonderful father to the girls and they had such an idyllic early childhood. When he died, I had to return to work and continued making hosiery for the firm until it closed in 1982. But, yes, things returned to normal very quickly. I was thankful for that. I wouldn't ever wish to relive those dark days of the war."

Nan never spoke that much about the death of her husband, so I declined to push any further. I nodded and decided to ask her one last question before pushing her back to Templars.

"And have you forgiven Di now?"

"Yes, I have. War makes us all do strange things. It took a long time though, but we did start to speak to each other at family occasions. I don't think either of us wanted to create a feud and have to lie to the rest of the family about why we weren't talking to each other. I think the distance between us, she living in Gloucester and myself in Baldock, helped heal the wound. We have always written to each other, and more recently telephoned. Family is too important to hold a grudge."

After I returned Nan to her room and fetched her a cup of tea, I was about to say goodbye when I paused and an idea entered my head.

"Aren't you curious to find out what happened to Brigitte?"

Nan looked up at me.

"I was for years, but it's been a long time now. I'm not sure I would want to know now, especially if she died. Probably better to let sleeping dogs lie."

I nodded and waved her goodbye. Nan had a point. Would she really want to know for sure this late in her life that she had killed Brigitte? But then if she hadn't killed her, then surely it would bring some inner peace. I examined the possibility that I could try to find out the truth. If it was bad news, then I would have to keep that information to myself.

Chapter 8

A few months later I had the answer that Nan wanted. I was very fortunate in that a former colleague of mine had a French-speaking wife who very generously gave up many hours of her time enquiring about Brigitte Duval. I was unsure how Nan would react to the news, so I decided to inform her within the confines of her own room.

"I hope you are not going to be annoyed, but I have some good news."

"Why would I be cross, when you have good news for me?" As sharp as ever, Nan had picked a gaping hole in my nonsensical statement.

"I've made a few enquiries and Brigitte survived." I paused to allow Nan to absorb the information.

"That's really good news," she took my hand and continued, "I'm so pleased. I knew that you would find out for me. Thank you."

"There's more. She has a daughter, who still lives in Étampes. She has invited us both to go and visit. She has something to show you."

"A visit to France? At my age?"

"Yes, we can go by train. It will take about six hours. I'm not expecting you to parachute in this time!"

"What has she got to show me?"

"Some papers and other stuff that belonged to her mother."

"Let me think about it."

I didn't push Nan any further, but in the meantime, someone had uploaded an old photograph of Grove House School to the Facebook page. Even more remarkable, it was dated as 1930, the exact time that Nan worked there. With a big grin on my face, I presented Nan with a printout of the photograph at the start of my next visit.

"Grove House School 1930," I stated triumphantly.

I could see that Nan was extremely pleased with my find, as she closely examined the print.

"Is that how you remember it?" I asked.

"Yes exactly," Nan smiled, "it doesn't seem that long ago really."

"It still looks the same today. Perhaps a little smarter, a lick of paint here and there, but otherwise it hasn't changed."

Since Nan had spoken about her times at Grove House, I had made a special effort to inspect the building more closely myself. Although today it is a private house, it really hasn't changed at all. The window frames look identical to the ones in the photograph and probably are.

"Can I keep it?" Nan asked.

"Of course, I printed it out for you." I answered.

"I've decided that I will make the journey back to Étampes."

I looked at Nan and smiled, unsure if she had made up her mind beforehand or whether the photograph had given her the final push to go; whichever it was I was truly delighted.

"Brilliant," I replied, "I shall start making arrangements.

Knowing that she hadn't killed Brigitte must have been a huge weight off her conscience. With that information she was able to make the trip, and in the subsequent days it became clear that she relished revisiting this part of her life. I had somewhat reluctantly agreed with her that we would tell the rest of the family that I was taking her to Gloucester to visit Di for a few days.

On the morning of departure Nan was very excited, and for once told Mrs Caunter the truth, knowing full well that she wouldn't believe her.

"Your Nan has such a wicked sense of humour," she laughed.

"Yes, I know. We're actually going to visit her sister in Gloucester."

"Yes, well you both have a good trip."

The first leg of our journey from Baldock to King's Cross would take around 40 minutes. I had suggested to Nan that we could break the journey by staying in a hotel once we had reached the Gare du Nord in Paris, but she was having none of it. It was almost as if she had shed ten years off her age since the trip was announced. One thing that I was extremely grateful for was the forecasted warm weather both here and in France. I don't think I would have managed to carry a heavy load of luggage full of blankets and jumpers, as well as pushing Nan in her wheelchair. I did consider embroiling my nephew in our plans, and although I'm sure he would have relished such subterfuge, I decided not to. The deception was bad enough, without dragging others into it!

"Do you know this will be the first time I have been on a train since the war?"

"Well, the trains are very different today." I replied.

"You mean they lack character," Nan corrected me, and as usual she was right.

"Such bland carriages," Nan remarked as we boarded the train at Baldock. With Nan's wheelchair safely folded away, we settled down as the train almost noiselessly crept out of the station. To our right we passed the Bogs, and on the left, the area of Baldock once nicknamed Hell's End.

"It's changed a lot, hasn't it?" I asked.

"Yes, very smooth and quiet," Nan replied.

"No, I meant Icknield Way, Hell's End."

"I know you did. Sorry, I was just being difficult. But yes, you are right. Apart from the cars parked everywhere it has changed for the better. Nobody should have had to live in those slums."

We were soon in London, and sitting aboard a Eurostar service in St Pancras station. I could sense that Nan was impressed with just how new and modern everything was now; the once run-down King's Cross area, the station interior, as well as the trains themselves. In fact, everything was a million miles away from the SNCF locomotives and carriages she so frequently journeyed on more than 70 years ago. I decided to limit the conversation, as I really wanted Nan to have a sleep. Despite her excitement and bravado, it was going to be a very long day for someone of her age. After we had been travelling for a short while, and the novelty of this futuristic train wore off, Nan dozed off and slept for most of the journey.

Once we had arrived in Paris, the dreaded transfer between the Gare du Nord and the Gare D'Austerlitz wasn't as horrid as I had feared. I knew Paris wasn't as wheelchair friendly as the UK, but Nan was happy to walk with her stick in the most challenging parts.

We were now on our way to Étampes. Nan, refreshed from her sleep, had come back to life again and was keenly eyeing the scenery from the window.

One of the many things I admire about France is her determination to stay in touch with her past and to avoid the bland modernisation that affects so many other countries; the UK perhaps being the epitome of this affliction.

Étampes station probably looked very much the same as it did in the 1940s, so I asked Nan for her expert opinion.

"Has it changed much?"

"No, not really. There's the telephone kiosk where I phoned from all those years ago."

We both stood looking around the station. Nan no doubt recalled those dark days of 70 years ago, while I was trying to imagine what it was like back then, and how remarkable that life carries on regardless of what has gone before.

"Right," Nan said, "shall we get going?"

"I'll find a taxi," I replied.

"Actually, would you mind if you pushed me in the wheelchair? I would like to see the town properly again."

"No, not at all. I could do with stretching my legs after the long train journey."

I unfolded the wheelchair and started to push Nan out of the station building.

"Stop," Nan called out as we entered the main street.

"What's the matter?" I asked, a little alarmed that Nan had changed her mind and didn't want to go through with the visit after all.

"Nothing, I just wanted to stop and observe the town. It hasn't changed as much as I thought it would have done. There's the bar I used to watch Brigitte come and go from the hospital. I had many excellent omelettes there! I don't suppose the same patron is there now. What am I talking about? He would be about 120 years old now!"

"Perhaps his son or daughter, or grandchildren run it now?" I suggested.

"Possibly."

"Do you want to go in?"

"Not now. Let's carry on to the house."

Some 15 minutes later, Nan indicated that we had arrived. She pointed across the road.

"The derelict building has gone."

What would have been a discarded shell the last time Nan was here was today a smart-looking residence with its recently-painted shutters and well-kept grounds. I then steered the wheelchair in the direction of Brigitte's old house.

"So has it changed much?"

"It's not so shabby now, but no it doesn't look very different at all."

The front door of the house opened as I negotiated the less-than-wheelchair-friendly terrain, and a woman in her sixties smiled and greeted us both.

"I'm so pleased to have you both here," she said.

"No, thank you for inviting us both into your home. It's very generous of you."

Gabrielle Duval had inherited her mother's confidence and self-assurance as Nan would tell me later. She also possessed her warmth and the same welcoming manner.

"Now Mrs Hill…" Gabrielle began to speak.

"Mabel please," Nan interjected.

"Mabel it is. Please call me Gaby. I've put you in a downstairs bedroom through there. Do you want to eat soon? Or do you want a rest or freshen up? It must have been a long and tiring journey."

"I think a quick freshen up and then some food. I do feel pretty hungry now." Nan looked at me to see if I agreed, to which I nodded.

"Excellent, shall we say half an hour's time?"

"Yes, suits me. Thank you." I replied.

Some 30 minutes later the three of us sat around the kitchen table tucking into a hearty vegetable stew along with some excellent crusty bread. So far, the conversation had been limited to small talk; our journey, Gaby's job, and her family. It turned out that Gaby worked in Etampes hospital. I wondered if it was the same one her mother had visited all those years ago.

"I must apologise, but I'm on a shift tonight. We are very short-staffed currently, and I couldn't get the time off."

"I'm sorry we've inconvenienced you."

"No, not at all. This is my last shift for three days, so I'm all yours from tomorrow. I'm sure you could both do with a good night's sleep anyway. My daughter Clara will be home soon. She will clear up, so please do not wash the dishes. She will also prepare your breakfast in the morning."

Despite my protestations, Gaby insisted that we were guests in her house, and would leave the clearing-up to her daughter.

"One last thing before I leave for work. I have here in this box my mother's diaries." Gaby lifted a large square box from the floor. "She kept a diary for most of her life. Tomorrow morning while I catch up on a few hours' sleep, please feel free to read some of them. Then we can catch up and talk about her."

I never sleep well in a strange bed on the first night, and despite the long day travelling, I probably grabbed about three hours sleep in total. In addition to the bed, there was undoubtedly a great deal of excitement and anticipation whirling around in my head about what tomorrow would bring. Nan, in contrast, commented on what a restful night's sleep she had.

After breakfast, once Gaby's equally delightful daughter had made herself scarce, I moved the rather heavy box of diaries onto the kitchen table once again. The diaries had been carefully placed in the box in chronological order with their spines facing upwards. The first one was dated 1930 and the last one 2005.

"The diaries stopped seven years ago," I remarked. "I assume that's when she died. So, if she was born in the same year as you, then she would have been 87 years old."

Nan nodded.

"Let's start with the 1930 diary. That's the year I first met Brigitte."

I withdrew the black leather-covered diary and opened the contents on the table so we could both see it. The neat sloping handwritten entries were entirely in French. Foolishly I hadn't expected this and knew that my own French could only extend to recognising certain words and phrases. Nan volunteered to read out loud the entries, translating as she went along. I was really very impressed at how fluent she was still, only hesitating very occasionally.

Sunday 2 March 1930, Grove House, Baldock

Welcome to my diary. My name is Brigitte Duval. I am 12 years old and come from Étampes, a small town south of Paris. I was given this diary as a Christmas present, but as you can see, I haven't used it for the first two months of the year. So why have I started using it you may ask? Well last month, my father who is a managing director of a screws and fastenings company was asked to come to England to help set up a factory near the town of Baldock where I am sitting writing this diary.

I'm not sure how long we will be staying, but my home for the foreseeable future is a room in Grove House boarding school. My bedroom is nice enough, but it is just one room, so I do feel a bit trapped and restless at times. There are seven other girls here, and we are allowed into each other's room but only until 8pm! Meals are at set times and lights out at 9pm. I'm not sure I will like it here. Lessons start tomorrow, so we shall see.

Monday 3 March 1930, Grove House, Baldock

I'm already bored with the lessons. The work was very easy. I have two teachers. Mrs Datchworth is the headmistress. She was very nice to Father when she was showing us both around last month, but in class I think she is going to be an absolute horror! Mrs Roberts is the other teacher. She seems much nicer. There are also two-day students in the class who go back to their own homes at the end of school. Lucky them!

Friday 7 March 1930, Grove House, Baldock

Well, my first week of school is over. I don't think I'm going to be best friends with any of the other girls. Most of them are quite snooty and standoffish with me, and being a foreigner makes it worse. There are two girls who are nicer than the rest, Dorothy (or Dot for short) and Elizabeth, but they are not very exciting to be with. All they want to do is study. Father is taking me out tomorrow, so perhaps I shall find out how long he thinks we will be staying in Baldock.

Saturday 8 March 1930, Grove House, Baldock

I am very sad today. Father called in this morning and cancelled because he has to go into work. He promised we will go out tomorrow. He left some money for me to go to the cinema which is just across the road from Grove House. There was a long war film on, so I bought some sweets and went for a walk instead. The only good thing about the week so far has been the mild and sunny weather.

Sunday 9 March 1930, Grove House, Baldock

I spent the day with Father. We walked around Baldock in the morning. It has a lovely old church, and we could hear the congregation singing hymns. It isn't a Catholic church though. It is called a Church of England. I don't think there is a Catholic church in Baldock, so I will try to persuade my father to take me another week to the Church of England. Most of the shops in Baldock are like the ones we have back in Étampes; butchers, bakers, greengrocers etc. Baldock also has something the English call a pub. What is a pub? It is a bit like a French bar in that it serves beer, but apart from that it is very different. Even the beer is different, it is dark beer not the light beer Father drinks at home. I don't think he likes it. Father took me to a pub.

Children under the age of 16 are not allowed inside, so I had to wait outside while he bought the drinks. I did look through the window though. Pubs are really old buildings and usually have oak beams. When Father came back with the drinks, we sat outside in the pub garden. What I really like about pubs is that they all have funny names, and each one has a sign outside with a picture and its name on it. We visited the White Lion where Father had rented a room. Some of the other pubs in Baldock are called the Bull's Head, the Queen Victoria, the White Hart, the Cock, and the Eight Bells. There are probably at least 25 pubs in Baldock. Next Sunday Father and I have been invited to have a traditional English roast dinner at a work colleague's house.

Friday 14 March 1930, Grove House, Baldock

I've nothing much to say this week. School lessons have been boring, and although Dot and Elizabeth are very nice, they are a bit dull. I don't think I shall be able to tempt them into having an adventure with me. I think the odd visit to the cinema is about their limit. There is a girl who cleans the school who seems to have a bit more about her. I heard Mrs Datchworth call her Mabel yesterday. I will try to make friends with her.

Saturday 15 March 1930, Grove House, Baldock

It rained all day today, so I decided to watch All Quiet on the Western Front at the cinema. It was very long and I surprised myself by actually enjoying it. Dot and Elizabeth didn't fancy it. Father visited late afternoon.

Sunday 16 March 1930, Grove House, Baldock

Today Father and I had lunch with a Mr Stanley Charter and his family. Mr Charter is going to be the works manager for the new factory. He and his wife have two young children aged six and four years old. They live in a lovely house on the High Street. Mrs Charter is lovely too, but I wasn't that keen on the traditional English roast dinner she served. To be honest everything was overcooked, especially the meat which was dry and barely edible. I lied when asked if I had enjoyed the meal. I just hope we're not invited every week!

Wednesday 19 March 1930, Grove House, Baldock

I spoke to Mabel for the first time today. I waited until she had completed all her cleaning duties and followed her out onto the street. She seemed very nervous when I first spoke to her, but I'm sure she was just worried that the horrid Mrs Datchworth would come out and tell her off. I only walked with her for five minutes, but I already know that we are going to be close friends. She has a lot more sparkle about her than the other girls.

Thursday 20 March 1930, Grove House, Baldock

I have been 'ill' today. The truth is Mrs Datchworth's Maths lesson was the most boring ever, so I faked an illness. She must have believed me, otherwise she wouldn't have sent me to the medical room. Once the nurse had seen me, I slipped out and sneaked up to my room. Of course, this was part of my elaborate plan to speak with Mabel. It was funny, she nearly jumped out of her skin when she entered my room to clean it! Anyway, I am meeting her after school tomorrow so she can show me around Baldock.

Friday 21 March 1930, Grove House, Baldock

Today I visited Mabel's house for the first time. So that we could spend more time together, I helped her get her chores done by peeling some potatoes and vegetables. Mabel is amazing, she goes to school all day, cleans at Grove House and still has time to do jobs at home. I'm not sure she gets that much time for herself. After we had finished, we walked around the town chatting. I have started to teach her some words in French. Tomorrow we are going to the pictures.

Saturday 22 March 1930, Grove House, Baldock

Had a really enjoyable afternoon with Mabel. We have a lot in common so we are going to meet as much as we can. Father called in later on. We have been invited to the Charters again for Sunday lunch. Groan!

Saturday 29 March 1930, Grove House, Baldock

Today Mabel took me to the Bogs (or the Marshes as some people call it). It is an incredible place and has everything we need for an adventure. There is a small river, marshes, a wood and a rubbish dump. Mabel is very knowledgeable about wildlife and showed me how to find the nests of several different species of birds. Her grandfather was a keen birdwatcher and passed his knowledge onto Mabel's older sister Di. She found a robin nesting in an old broken metal watering can that had slipped off one of the rubbish tips and ended up in some vegetation. It's such a genius place to nest, I would have never have thought of looking there. Another day Mabel is going to show me how to catch frogs and newts. We will also start looking for somewhere to build a hideaway, which will be our own special place where no else can visit.

Saturday 5 April 1930, Grove House, Baldock

I am really enjoying my time in Baldock now. School is now bearable because I can spend time with Mabel after school and on weekends when I am not with my father. I am doing so many new and different things. Today Mabel showed me how to catch frogs and newts. Frogs are very tricky to catch, and it often takes several attempts. When we caught them, we put them in old glass jars we found at the dump, but at the end of the day we returned them to the wild. I caught two frogs and nine newts. Not bad but Mabel caught nearly twice as many!

We have also found a good place to build our hideaway. We are going to start collecting material to build it next week.

Saturday 12 April 1930, Grove House, Baldock

It has been a really busy week. Every spare opportunity Mabel and I have had, we have been collecting material for our hideaway. The rubbish dump is full of interesting things. I'm surprised we don't ever see any other children here, because it is such an amazing place to play. The only visitor is the occasional truck which dumps more rubbish, but that is not very often. When we hear them coming, we hide since I don't suppose we are allowed here really. We now have quite a collection of material. It has taken ages to carry it all over to the site of our hideaway. We have pieces of metal, scraps of wood and old sacking for the shell, and for the inside we have found an old table, glass bottles for putting things in and some old crates which we can make into seats. I am also going to buy some candles that we can stick in some of the glass bottles.

Nan paused for a break so that I could brew some coffee.

"You certainly made a very good impression on her," I commented.

"Yes, we did get on very well."

"Does it bring it all back to you?"

"Yes, it doesn't seem like over 80 years ago. They were good times. I really want to find out why she left Baldock all of a sudden."

Once we had finished our coffee, Nan flicked through the next few months of the diary.

"The next set of entries are mostly concerned with our hideaway we built. Here's the last day I saw her in Baldock."

Friday 11 July 1930, Grove House, Baldock

Yesterday's dummy run was perfect. I do hope I'm not being too forceful with Mabel, but she's a clever girl, I know that she can do it. It is 8.30pm now and shortly I will be meeting Mabel so that we can spend the night in our hideaway. I am very excited; I hope everything goes well!

Nan broke off, "No entry for Saturday 12 July or for the next day. Something definitely happened. Here's an entry for the following Monday."

Monday 14 July 1930, Hotel Marylebone, London

As you can probably tell something happened. I went to meet Mabel on Friday evening, but she didn't show up. I hope she wasn't caught climbing out of her window. I think she would get into a lot of trouble if she was caught, and it would be all my fault for persuading her. Anyway, it was a good thing I was at Grove House on Saturday morning because Father was taken ill. It is quite bad as he has been taken to a hospital in London, and I still don't know if he is going to be alright. Mrs Charter has accompanied me to London, where we are staying in a hotel. It is really very decent of her, because she has two young children of her own. I understand her mother is looking after them. I had to leave Grove House

164

very quickly. I couldn't leave a letter for Mabel, because if Mrs Datchworth found it first, she would get into trouble, so I've left my French-English dictionary for her to find. I'm sure she will find it. I just hope she doesn't think Mrs Datchworth caught me sneaking out Friday night, and had thrown me out of school. Hopefully Father will be alright and I can return to Grove House. It will be sad if I don't see Mabel again.

Nan stopped reading and replaced the diary on the table.

"Poor Brigitte. How horrible for her."

"But you did find her dictionary."

"Yes, we understood each other totally."

I could sense Nan was quite emotional as she seemingly wiped a tear from her eye.

Nan picked the diary back up and started to look through the next set of entries. She then breathed a sigh of relief, "Yes, good news. Her father made a full recovery and they went back to France."

Nan closed the diary and laid it down onto the table. Behind us the door to the stairs opened and in walked Gaby. Looking refreshed after her snooze, she had now joined both of us at the kitchen table.

"How are you getting on?"

"Very well, absolutely fascinating," I replied.

"Do you feel like taking a break, we can go out into the garden. It's such a lovely day."

As a sun worshipper Nan needed no persuading, although with the temperature at around 30°C even she eventually joined Gaby and me in the shade under a large ash tree. Once

Gaby had organised some refreshments, she asked Nan if the diaries made sense.

"Yes, it seems like yesterday that Brigitte and I were engaging in our adventures."

"Mabel, my mother told me very little about her childhood, and even less about what she did in the war."

I could see Nan look a little uneasy when Gaby mentioned Brigitte's involvement in the war, but she appeared not to notice and carried on speaking.

"It's only recently that I found the diaries and read them. It sounds as if she had a fascinating life. I would love to hear more about it from someone who was there."

Nan nodded and asked me to fetch her handbag from inside the house. She took the bag from me and carefully drew out an envelope which I immediately realised contained the old photographs of Baldock that I had printed out from the Facebook page.

"This photo is of Grove House School."

Gaby peered forward and studied the old photograph.

"This room was your mother's." Nan pointed to the far left-hand-side window on the first floor.

"This is fascinating Mabel. Thank you so much for bringing it."

"And this is the cinema. We spent many happy afternoons there."

"It's amazing. It's like bringing my mother back to life."

After showing Gaby the photograph of FW Cooper's butcher with 'les cochons' hanging outside, Nan presented the print of Church Street.

"This is where I lived, and where we were to meet on the evening before her father, your grandfather, was taken ill. I was very nearly caught climbing out of my bedroom to meet your mother."

Nan continued to explain to Gaby what had happened that night, how she had woken her parents by crashing into the bathtub, and failed to keep her rendezvous with Brigitte. Gaby had many more questions about her mother's childhood for Nan, who happily relived her halcyon days to the sheer delight of Gaby. Nearly an hour had passed, when Gaby looked at her watch.

"I'm sorry Mabel, I'm getting carried away here. You must be exhausted with all the travelling yesterday and now me with my continual questioning. You must have a break now."

"No, I'm fine," insisted Nan, but I decided to step in and take an unusually firm hand with her.

"You must have a break, Nan. You may feel OK, but all this exertion will catch up with you soon. You don't want to be exhausted for the rest of your stay."

"Very well then, but I've only been sitting on a train, and talking. It's hardly strenuous exercise."

This was Nan's way of accepting I had a point. She wouldn't ever admit it, but she knew she needed a rest and would have resisted otherwise.

"Have a rest, and then I'll make some lunch, or if you feel up to it, we could go into Étampes. Don't decide now, see how you feel later."

Nan was obviously more tired than she had let on, for when I went to check on her a couple of hours later, she was still asleep. When she did emerge from her room some two and a half hours after entering it, I sensed she was still putting on a front for Gaby's benefit.

"That's better. I feel refreshed now," she stated.

"Would you like some lunch?" Gaby asked. It was nearly three o'clock and I had already eaten.

"Yes please," replied Nan.

"What would you like? I have some delicious bread and cheese. I hear you're a big fan of cheese."

I smirked at Gaby as she addressed Nan.

"Yes please. Is it that lovely hard cheese? I remember enjoying it when I was last here."

"Yes, Cantal," Gaby replied, displaying a sizeable lump of the stuff in her hand.

While Gaby was preparing her lunch, I asked Nan what she wanted to do for the rest of the day.

"I've been thinking. It is probably best if I read some more diaries first, certainly the 1940 and 1941 ones when I was last here. I can then read through Brigitte's side of things before I answer any questions that Gaby has."

Nan looked over to Gaby as she brought a plate of freshly cut bread and cheese over to the table.

"I need to do that before we talk more or visit the town to see my old haunts. Perhaps if we could do that this afternoon, and then we can talk this evening?"

Gaby nodded, "Yes, that's a good idea, but only if you are not too tired. I've some errands to run this afternoon, so I can leave you to it."

Not only was Gaby an excellent host, but very tactful too in making herself scarce for the rest of the afternoon.

Once Gaby had left, I questioned Nan about how tired she was feeling.

"I'm fine. I was tired earlier I admit, but I really am OK now."

"I think I would like to have a look at her diaries from the war period next."

I carefully replaced the 1930 diary in its correct position and withdrew the diaries dated 1939, 1940 and 1941.

"Which one do you want to start with?" I asked.

"1940 of course. That's when Germany invaded France."

Nan flicked through the diary until she came across the entry she required.

"Here we are."

23 May 1940, Étampes

The Germans have reached Paris which means it will only be a matter of days before they reach Étampes. I have joined a local resistance group. We had our first meeting last night to come up with some ideas about what we can do once the Germans arrive.

26 May 1940, Étampes

The Germans entered Étampes today. They may have arrived without a struggle, but we will give them one hell of a fight until they have been beaten and sent packing. Father says he expects them to take over our factory within days. The Germans have already introduced a night time curfew. Everybody has to be inside by dusk and then not out again until 5am the following morning. They have also taken down the tricolour at the town hall and replaced it with the flag of the Third Reich.

27 May 1940, Étampes

It's official, our family business is now providing munitions for the Germans. Father is to stay in charge, so we are collaborators! I am worried about his health; I think the stress may cause a relapse. How I hate the Germans.

29 May 1940, Étampes

I attended the first meeting of our resistance group since the Germans took over the town. We have lots of ideas about how to disrupt the invaders. I am in charge of sabotaging the munitions at my father's factory, but I am worried the Germans may take it out on him if the production is disrupted. We have heard some stories from Paris that when sabotage attacks against the occupiers take place, they round up 20 random people off the streets and start to kill them one by one each day until the perpetrators are found or give themselves up. I don't care if they capture me, I am willing to sacrifice myself for France. I need to formulate a really good plan.

3 June 1940, Étampes

Life at the factory is already unbearable. There is so much pressure on my father to increase production. The workforce has become slave labour. In terms of sabotage, the Germans have eyes everywhere, so it is going to be very difficult to hinder production.

7 June 1940, Étampes

Met up with fellow resistance members last night. They have a plan to attack the aerodrome and want me to get some bombs from the factory. I'm not sure how I can do this, but I said I would try. It may take some time though.

13 June 1940, Étampes

I have worked out a plan to smuggle some bomb-making equipment out of the factory. It will take some time, but my fellow resistance members are impressed with my dedication. So am I. It will require getting friendly with one of the German guards. I feel sick just thinking about it!

14 June 1940, Étampes

I think I have identified the soldier I will befriend. Actually, he is very nice, always polite and quite good-looking. It will perhaps make it a bit easier if I have to go out with him. In the meantime, I am bending over backwards to be as co-operative as possible in helping Father run the factory efficiently and increasing production, and hopefully showing that we can be good collaborators!

26 June 1940, Étampes

I am getting on very well with Private Oberhost, or Ludwig as he insists on being called. He has already asked me out for a drink with him. I managed to put him off, but I know I will have too sooner or later. I will just have to develop some broad shoulders because those who don't know what I am part of, will brand me a collaborator, slut, whore and worse. So, the first stage of my plan is well under way.

27 June 1940, Étampes

The second phase of my plan started to fall into place today. Before the Germans arrived, I shared an office with my father, but as we are busier, I had one of the old storerooms cleared out to create an office for me to use. Today I had some furniture delivered, although much to the amusement of the Germans it is too large to go through the office door, and currently sits outside on the factory floor. Obviously, it will have to be returned and some smaller items ordered instead. Unbeknown to the Germans the furniture was deliberately made too big and has many secret compartments within it, to store items such as bomb-making equipment!

It is still going to be difficult to find opportunities to hide material in the furniture, but far easier than trying to smuggle stuff out bit by bit, which actually has become impossible with the stringent searches that take place each time we leave. How do you like my own version of the Trojan horse?

4 July 1940, Étampes

My Trojan horse (or horses – as there are several pieces of furniture) are gradually being filled with bomb-making equipment for the attack on the aerodrome. I have decided to go out with Private Oberhost tomorrow night. I explained to him I didn't want to be seen out with him for fear of reprisals. He was very sweet about it and is taking me somewhere quiet where I hopefully will not be recognised. I have agreed to go out with him because I need to initiate the next part of my plan.

5 July 1940, Étampes

Private Oberhost was the perfect gentleman on our first 'date'. I explained to him I have decided to keep the furniture, but want it sent to my house. He is going to organise some transport to take my Trojan horses there! It's a perfect plan, the Germans will never suspect.

Father's health seems to have improved a little, even though he worries what will happen to me if I am caught.

9 July 1940, Étampes

The Trojan horses were moved out of the factory today. It was a good job I had Oberhost on side as the gate guard seemed reluctant to allow the furniture to leave without any paperwork. Over the next few nights, the Resistance members will move the equipment to some caves in a wooded area south of the aerodrome.

16 July 1940, Étampes

All of the bombs have been assembled and a plan to attack the aerodrome has been finalised. We now have to wait for a cloudy night, so we have less chance of being detected. Most of the party will lie low in the caves once the deed has been done, until the furore has died down. There are a few of us, myself included, who will be missed the next morning if we fail to show for work. Therefore, we have an escape route by bike along back paths. We should get back to the town easily enough without being detected.

Food prices are starting to increase now, and some foodstuffs are becoming increasingly scarce. Meats seem to be in short supply, although you can always seem to get some if you pay an inflated price or go to the best restaurants in town. There is a lot of resentment building up as some locals are being accused of being collaborators. I know from experience that it is unpleasant to be accused, but if they are, then they deserve it. I'm willing to give them the benefit of the doubt though, as they may well be giving that impression, but secretly working against the Germans like I am.

24 July 1940, Étampes

Yesterday's attack on the aerodrome seemed to go well. We are waiting for confirmation of the exact damage, but there are certainly a few angry-looking Germans patrolling the factory this morning. I'm not sure that they can suspect the bombs came from this factory with all the checks they carry out. I shall try to garner some information from Oberhost later.

Oberhost told me over 30 planes were destroyed. He tells me that 20 locals are going to be rounded up and killed unless those responsible give themselves up. He advised me to avoid the town centre for the next 24 hours. I suppose I should be grateful to him, if only he knew! I do feel very bad for those that will be captured though.

In the following weeks a number of our members were captured and killed. I'm really sorry for them and their families, but it just makes me want to do more. We shall regroup and plan more attacks.

28 July 1940, Étampes

Disaster has struck the factory. It was bombed last night during an allied air raid. The explosions that resulted woke up the whole town. The factory was totally destroyed. I have mixed feelings. It has cut off a supply of munitions for the enemy, but it is Father's livelihood that he had toiled hard during the whole of his working life. He is devastated.

30 July 1940, Étampes

I met with resistance members last night. We celebrated our attack, although a couple of our members have been arrested by the Gestapo already. We have decided to lie low for a while. With the factory gone, I have been earmarked for a new role. I am going to be a guide for the escape line, returning British RAF aircrew to the UK. It sounds really exciting.

Nan stopped reading to have another break. She said what I was thinking.

"It doesn't sound as if Brigitte was a collaborator to me. She is so brave and such a patriot. I can't understand why she gave information to the Germans about the movement of aircrew."

"I have a feeling we shall find the answer in these pages."

"Yes," Nan replied, trying in vain to suppress a huge yawn.

I regarded Nan, sensing that she was very eager to find the answer. I didn't want to nag her incessantly about having a rest, so I settled on a compromise.

"Yes, I'm feeling tired too. Let's have a break, then after dinner we can return to them if you're feeling up to it."

Nan gave me a rueful look, perhaps suggesting that I had turned the tables on her this time.

"Very well then," she replied, "let's have a break."

It was quite late when the four of us, (Gaby's daughter Clara had joined us), tucked into the evening meal. The conversation revolved around the present with Nan asking both Gaby and Clara about their work. It turned out that Clara, like her mother, was a nurse at Étampes hospital.

"Shall we adjourn to the garden and continue our chat about Mum's diaries out there?" Gaby suggested, "It's still very warm out."

I looked at Nan, who nodded.

"I'll get a blanket from your room just in case," I added.

"Right, I'll brew some coffee and bring out some nice cheeses too." Gaby said as she rose from the table and cleared the last pieces of dirty crockery and cutlery.

The setting orangey sun glowed deeply as it sank towards the horizon, casting ever-lengthening shadows across Gaby's Garden from the tall cedar trees that lined the boundary of the property.

"I do love France," I stated, "it's just so tranquil and so quiet compared to back home. Listen."

Nan listened, a little confused that she couldn't hear anything.

"What? I can't hear anything."

"That's it. No distant drone of traffic from the A1 motorway. Just serenity."

Gaby had now joined us and placed on the table a tray with a pot of coffee and a selection of cheeses. Nan tucked into the cheeses almost immediately. I was glad that she was eating well.

"So where have you got to with the diaries?" Gaby asked as she handed us our coffees.

"Your grandfather's factory has just been bombed, and your mother is going to be a guide for the escape line," I replied while Nan filled her face with cheese.

"She was incredibly brave to help sabotage the airfield. You must be very proud of her." Nan added as gobbled down the cheese.

"Yes, I am," Gaby replied.

"Tell me, what happened to the factory? Was it rebuilt? And your grandfather, what happened to him?"

This time it was Gaby's turn to inform Nan of the events that had occurred, rather than the other way round. Gaby explained to Nan that the factory was never rebuilt by her grandfather, and today a supermarket stands on the site. His health did recover to a certain extent but not enough to withstand the stress of running a factory on a day-to-day basis. Fortunately, he had enough money saved to support himself and Brigitte, so he didn't work again. He died in 1960 aged 75 years old, which was far beyond what Brigitte had expected.

"I can show you the site of the factory when we go into Étampes tomorrow."

"That's quite a coincidence. Kayser Bondor is a supermarket today too." I remarked to Nan.

"Do you want to go into Étampes town tomorrow, Mabel?" Gaby asked.

"Yes, can we go tomorrow afternoon? That will give us a chance to read the next set of diary entries. The ones where we were both in Étampes at the same time."

"Good, I shall look forward to it," Gaby replied.

I was glad that Nan didn't insist on ploughing through any more entries that night, and after a couple of more yawns she retired to bed without any complaints. Tomorrow was probably going to be an emotionally and potentially physically exhausting day for her.

Chapter 9

My second night in France was much more comfortable in terms of sleep, having got very little during the previous one. Despite the warmth of the night, the reflectivity of the white-washed outer walls of the house permitted surprisingly cool and pleasant sleeping conditions. Consequently, I rose much later than I normally would have done. Gaby, not surprisingly as a perfect host, was already up and preparing breakfast.

"Morning, did you have a good night's sleep?" she asked, smiling as she did so.

"Yes, very good thank you. The room stays nice and cool in the heat."

"Yes, they all do, but they can be very cold in the winter!" Gaby smiled once again. "I've set up breakfast outside. It's another lovely day, will Mabel be OK with that?"

"I'm sure she will. I'll go and see if she is awake yet."

Nan, looking refreshed from her night's sleep, joined both of us outside for breakfast. As a sun-worshipper Nan needed no persuading to sit outside, although as the temperatures rose during the course of the morning, she eventually joined me under the shade of a large ash tree. After breakfast Gaby left the two of us to continue with the reading of the diaries.

12 August 1940, Étampes

I made my first journey down the escape line today. I accompanied an experienced guide to show me the ropes. We successfully escorted two aircrew from Étampes to Tours. Although it passed off very smoothly with no incidents it was still very exciting because you are on edge for the whole of the journey. You never know when your papers will be checked. Then the adrenalin really starts to flow as you wonder if you will dupe the Germans into believing that they are bona fide.

19 August 1940, Étampes

I escorted two aircrew down the escape line on my own for the very first time today. I was a bag of nerves, but it all passed off very successfully. There is a huge German presence, but they don't seem to have a clue what is going on.

I could sense that Nan was very eager to find out the answer, as she rather impatiently began to flick through and scan the pages of Brigitte's diary. Nan had advanced a couple of months when she stopped and appeared to have found what she was looking for.

3 October 1940, Étampes

I had to pull out of a mission today. Father has not been well for some time now and was rushed into hospital. He has lost a lot of weight and looks quite frail. I am really worried about him. The stress of losing the factory and this war is not helping.

10 October 1940, Étampes

Today has probably been the worst day of my life. I had just returned from visiting Father in hospital when there was a knock at the front door. Standing there was an officer of the Gestapo. He was slimy for sure, but as far as Gestapo officers go, he seemed more civilised than most. The fact that he was almost pleasant, surely meant that he had no idea I was helping with the escape line, and actually if that was the case, I would have been hauled down to Gestapo headquarters, locked in a cell, and tortured.

He is essentially blackmailing me. He pointed out that both Father and I were good collaborators when the factory was in operation. He has promised that Father will receive better treatment if I find out about any escape line! So, what can I do? He might be lying about the treatment, but Father is seriously ill. He has given me 24 hours to decide. I'm not going to mention it to Father, as I know what his answer will be – 'tell the Germans to go to hell!' I'm sure I will have a sleepless night tonight.

11 October 1940, Étampes

I have made my decision, and I hate myself for it, but Father is the only close relative I have left in this world. I have decided I will feed the Gestapo officer a few crumbs of information. It will mean sacrificing some airmen, but hopefully the Luftwaffe police will see them become prisoners of war, and not end up being tortured by the Gestapo. Anyway, the aircrew won't be able to disclose many details about the escape line because we are so careful. Am I doing the right thing? One thing I am sure about is that this

Gestapo officer is a lone wolf. I believe he is working on his own and trying to impress his superiors with as many scoops as he can. The trouble is I don't know when the aircrew are being sent down the line (apart from the ones I escort), so I am going to have to sit around at the station watching for activity, as well as visiting father and running the house. What a mess!

16 October 1940, Étampes

I almost betrayed my first set of aircrews today. I spotted them at the station, but as there were three of them, I decided not to. I am only going to make tip-offs about parties of one or two aircrew.

21 October 1940, Étampes

I made my first phone call to the Gestapo agent today. I spotted two aircrew getting onto a train with a guide. I waited until the train departed, and then made the call from the station telephone kiosk. How am I going to live with myself? And what am I going to do if the agent starts to demand more?

Nan placed the diary down once again.

"Poor Brigitte, being blackmailed by the Gestapo."

"What a predicament," I stated. "What would you have done in her situation?"

"Probably the same. It's just horrible."

Nan started turning the next pages in the diary, shaking her head.

"Another one. She is at her wit's end."

21 November 1940, Étampes

I had to tell Father the truth today. He has sensed for some time now that something has been bothering me. Father said I had to stop immediately, but the thing is he is responding to the treatment. I can't let him go back to how he was. I know he is probably right and that I will eventually compromise the whole escape line. He agrees with me that the Gestapo agent is a lone wolf, otherwise I would be in custody by now. So, I have made a compromise with him, and have agreed to stop once he is well enough to leave the hospital.

Nan read out some more entries detailing Brigitte's betrayals and the increasing pressure the Gestapo office placed upon her, even threatening to withdraw the treatment. We had reached the part of the story where Nan had followed Brigitte.

"This is the date that I followed her for the first time. If only it hadn't been a wet day, and then I would have been able to recognise her and help her."

"You might have placed yourself in even more danger," I suggested.

"I disagree. What I was doing was dangerous anyway. We could have come up with a plan and prevented the capture of the aircrew."

I nodded in agreement.

8 July 1941, Étampes

Estelle arrived with the produce and a new message for me today. I am to escort two aircrew down the line tomorrow. The recent fine weather has given way to thunderstorms and heavy rain. I went to see Father. He is so much better and should be leaving the hospital soon. I'm very worried what the Gestapo officer will do next. I have a feeling I will have to keep acting as a mole for him, otherwise he will just have me arrested. I don't know what to do.

9 July 1941, Étampes

I delivered the two aircrew down the escape line today. I thought I might have had a tail for part of the way to the station, but it may have just been my imagination. A girl in a mac and headscarf was walking some way behind me as I entered the town, but I'm fairly certain she didn't board the train. It must have been a coincidence otherwise the aircrew would have been arrested. If the Gestapo agent is a lone wolf, then he can't possibly follow me 24 hours a day.

14 July 1941, Étampes

The Gestapo man visited again today. He is getting greedier and expects me to feed him information even when I haven't got anything to give. He keeps reminding me that my father could easily have a relapse. He is basically threatening to murder my father unless I co-operate. I will have to visit the station more often and see if I can spot any more aircrew.

20 July 1941, Étampes

Regrettably I have informed the Gestapo agent of more aircrew at Étampes station. I have got to end this, but how? Perhaps Father and I could run away together?

Obviously at this stage Brigitte was at her wit's end. Nan found the entry on the night she shot the Gestapo officer and Brigitte.

22 July 1941, Étampes

I barely slept last night. I still can't believe what has happened and that I am here to write this entry. I should perhaps be dead or arrested, but I am alive. I thank God.

Last night the Gestapo officer visited me at the house to put pressure on me to give him more information (the aircrew I tipped him off about somehow managed to evade capture). While we were speaking, a loud crash originated from outside. The Gestapo officer went to investigate and he was shot dead. I then came face to face with his killer. Incredibly it was Mabel, the English girl I last saw in Baldock over ten years ago! I think she was going to shoot me, but I must have fainted as when I woke up, the only injury I had was a graze on the arm. I'm sure she wasn't that bad a shot, after all she had just killed the Gestapo officer. He was dead, but Mabel was nowhere to be seen. Believing my hunch to be a correct one, regarding the officer being a lone wolf, I dug a hole and buried him. I think I would have been arrested by now if his headquarters knew he was visiting me. I am going to visit Father later. I think I will have to tell him what has happened. He will know what to do next.

23 July 1941, Étampes

Father was so pleased to see me; he obviously knew something had happened. It turns out that someone from the escape line visited him yesterday to ask him about me. He came clean and told the woman everything. I think he probably saved my life. I am wondering if it was Mabel who discovered my betrayal and asked for the matter to be checked out, although she did seem as shocked as I was. She must have deliberately missed and spared my life.

Nan stopped reading and started to weep. I had never seen her cry like this before.

"All these years I thought I had killed her, and all these years Brigitte thought I had spared her."

"I know," I put my arm around Nan to comfort her.

"And all these years I felt resentment towards Di for not passing on that message. As it turns out it was a stroke of luck, Brigitte fainting, that saved her life."

"No, I disagree. You may have subconsciously missed, and you did check her pulse. If you really meant to kill her you could have done so."

"I didn't call for a doctor or ambulance though."

"That's because you wanted to protect others in the escape line. You were under enormous pressure, and actually it has all worked out well in the end. Even if it has taken over 70 years for the story to come out."

"Yes, I suppose it has."

It suddenly crossed my mind that the Gestapo officer was buried somewhere in the grounds of the property. I looked at Nan, unsure if I should say anything, but it was Nan who spoke next.

"You're thinking what I'm thinking aren't you?" Nan looked out across the garden.

"Yes," I replied, "does it bother you?"

"No, it happened a long time ago. I don't suppose anyone knows where exactly he is buried."

"Are you OK to talk with Gaby now? I'll go and fetch her if you are."

"Yes, I shall be fine. I'm just so pleased Brigitte wasn't a traitor."

Gaby joined us both shortly and asked how we had fared with the diaries. I looked at Nan waiting for her to respond. I wasn't sure how much she wanted to tell Gaby about what had happened. Never one to tell lies unnecessarily, Nan stuck to the truth and admitted it was more down to luck than judgement that Brigitte had survived that night.

"Mabel, I am a great believer in fate. I know that you were unaware of her being blackmailed, but those above you did and in a way that spared her. Had they not spoken to my grandfather, she would almost certainly have been killed by those in charge of the escape line. So as far as I'm concerned you saved her life."

"That's what I said," I chipped in with my own viewpoint, "and you probably subconsciously weren't trying to kill her as much as you were when you aimed the gun at the Gestapo officer."

"And you got that awful Gestapo officer off her back and saved more aircrew from being captured," Gaby added.

Perhaps not concurring totally, Nan nodded and desisted from disagreeing any further.

Nan shifted in her seat and appeared to hesitate before she spoke next.

"I don't suppose you know where he is buried?"

"No, I don't. It's funny though, when my father and grandfather died, money was really tight for years, but my mother was adamant that we would never sell up and move into a smaller house. I think she was protecting you somehow, although what you did was a perfectly legitimate action."

"Knowing Brigitte, she would have thought of a good place to bury him and conceal the spot well."

Simultaneously we all glanced around the garden until our eyes fell upon a large and unruly honeysuckle.

"It's a possibility," I suggested.

Keen to move on, Nan enquired what had happened to Brigitte after the war.

"So, what happened to your mother after the war? We haven't reached those diaries yet."

Gaby described how her mother had trained to be a nurse at Étampes hospital after the war had ended. It was there that she met her husband, Gérard, who was a doctor there. They married after a very short engagement and Gaby was born in late 1948. Three years later her brother was stillborn, and greater tragedy struck the family when her father died at the age of 36 when Gaby was only six years old. Despite this she enjoyed an idyllic childhood and was particularly fond of her grandfather whose house it was. He died in 1960 leaving just Brigitte and Gaby to oversee the running of the property. They often struggled to make ends meet, but Gaby was able to follow in her mother's footsteps and trained to become a nurse, which brought in a second wage. Gaby got married in 1972 and Clara was born six years later in 1978.

Likewise, Nan gave a brief family history which bore some resemblance to Brigitte's; getting married in 1939, giving birth to three daughters, and losing her husband soon after they were born.

Once the two of them had finished swapping micro-biographies, Gaby asked Nan where she would like to visit this afternoon.

"Let's go for lunch in the bar opposite the station, I see it is still there. It will be strange to sit in there again after all these years, but fun to do. And also, let's all walk along the main street so I can retrace my steps."

"There is one other place I would like to take you as well." Gaby looked at me, and then to Nan.

"There is something I haven't told you, but my mother is still alive. I didn't tell you before because I didn't want to get you over here on false pretences. You will have noticed that the diaries end in 2005." We both nodded, still reeling from what Gaby had just said. "My mother has Alzheimer's. As someone who had such a logical brain and always thought for herself, Brigitte has effectively been dead these past two years. She was initially diagnosed eight years ago. The disease accelerated quickly at first before slowing, and for the past five years she has been in a nursing home. In the last two years she has lost just about all of her memory. I'm lucky now if she recognises me once or twice a month. I go to see her every day, but it is often painful seeing a loved one not know who you are. I didn't want to get you over here when I knew in all probability she wouldn't recognise or remember you. I hope you understand."

I nodded, as did Nan.

"Of course. We understand totally. It has been wonderful for Nan just to read her diaries," I replied.

"Will you take me to see her?" asked Nan.

"Of course. We can go later this afternoon if that suits."

189

Later that afternoon the three of us made the 15-minute journey to the Étampes town centre. Gaby and I walked, with Nan in her wheelchair.

"Well has it changed much?" I asked Nan as we sat down in the bar that she had last visited over 70 years ago. Now called Pascal's, Nan tried to remember what it was called back then, but much to her annoyance she couldn't quite recollect.

"Not really," she replied scanning the bar, noting the still-spartan furniture and décor, "apart from the mod-cons, it's pretty much as I remember it."

I picked up a menu from the table and grinned as I immediately recognised the dish 'Omelette au fromage' listed.

"I think I know what you will be having. I will have the same."

"Let's make that three cheese omelettes and coffees in Mabel's honour." Gaby concluded.

Nan smiled, and then took a few moments to reflect by peering outside into the street.

"It seems strange," Nan mused, "you would never have thought such death and destruction ravaged these streets 70 years ago."

Gaby and I allowed Nan some further time to reflect before the food arrived.

After lunch and some further sightseeing, the three of us walked for five short minutes to Étampes nursing home. The building was once a hotel, Gaby pointed out, which explained the wide corridors. It had been converted during the last decade, which accounted for the good condition of the décor. We passed a communal lounge which had a large flat-screen TV blaring out what appeared to be a French soap opera.

"I expect even you can hear that?" I asked Nan.

"What?" she replied with a big grin.

None of the residents appeared to be watching the programme; in fact, most were asleep. It is perhaps relatively easy to feel a little depressed at the sight of so many old people fading away in such places, but I always prefer to focus on the many wonderful and interesting lives people from Nan's generation have lived. From here we took the lift to the second floor.

Brigitte's room was surprisingly spacious, with a view overlooking the town's railway station. She would have walked the route to the railway station and beyond to the hospital many times as a young girl and since. I wondered if Brigitte had any recollection of using the station during the war when she was a guide for the escape line. If she didn't, then I thought the chances of her remembering Nan were close to zero.

The room itself was cheery enough with a couple of watercolour paintings hung on the cream-coloured walls. There was a small cabinet next to the window with several photographs in assorted frames dotted across the surface. One of them was possibly Brigitte as a young girl with her father, mother and sister, before the latter two were killed. Again, I wondered if she knew who they were.

"Mother, I've brought someone to see you."

Brigitte was much frailer than Nan and certainly looked like her 94 years. She looked at Gaby, but did not reply.

"Mother, look I've brought someone to see you."

Brigitte appeared to have very little comprehension of what her daughter had just said, and continued to gaze straight ahead, blissfully unaware that there were an additional two people in the room.

I carefully wheeled Nan as close as I could to Brigitte. This time Brigitte did look up, but there still appeared to be no look of recognition on her face. This was hardly surprising since 70 years had passed since they last saw each other. Gaby bent down and tried once more to grab her mother's attention.

"This is Mabel Ellis from Baldock."

It was evident, as Gaby had explained back at the house, that it was extremely unlikely that Brigitte's memory would be reignited.

It was Nan who initiated the next attempt by taking out of her handbag the photograph of Grove House School and handing it to Brigitte. Brigitte peered down at the picture, but gave no indication that she recognised it. I could sense that Gaby was a little disappointed, as I was. Nan just smiled though and surprised both Gaby and I by withdrawing a book from the side of her wheelchair. She opened the book and placed it on Brigitte's lap. Brigitte looked down at the book and began to read some words which were written inside.

"M, I've had to go away. All my love B x".

Brigitte smiled at Mabel, and took her hand.

"Mabel."

Nan smiled back and gently squeezed Brigitte's hand.

"You remember me then?"

"Yes, I never found out why you didn't meet me?"

I glanced over at Gaby whose pleasure was evident.

"It was a dark night and I crashed into our metal bathtub. I had to quickly get back into bed before Father caught me! I'm sorry."

192

"No, don't be. My father was rushed to hospital. Do you know how he is?"

"He's fine. He's going to be alright."

Nan smiled again and glanced up at Gaby to check that she had said the right thing. Gaby nodded and smiled.

Nan and Brigitte continued to talk about their time together in Baldock when they were both young girls. It was evident that Brigitte had no recollection of her wartime activities, so Nan didn't broach the subject.

Once we had left the room, Nan spoke.

"I'd like to visit again tomorrow before we leave."

"That would be fantastic," Gaby replied, "and thank you so much Mabel for bringing those memories back to her. It was so heart-warming to hear her talk about her childhood."

When we departed the next day, Gaby invited us both back the next summer for as long as we wanted so that we could finish reading the diaries and visit Brigitte. It was an emotional farewell at the station, especially given the history of it for both Nan and Gaby's family.

None of us were really sure we would ever be back, but I was very thankful I had made this, the longest travel with my Nan.

Epilogue

May 2013, Baldock

Less than a year after our visit to Étampes, Gaby telephoned me one overcast, chilly March morning to break the sad news that Brigitte had passed away. It appeared that the brief upturn in her mental and physical health, following Nan's visit, had subsided and was no more than one final flicker in Brigitte's long and eventful life.

I dreaded breaking the news to Nan, but as I was the only member of the family who had met Brigitte, I felt it was my duty to do so. I would have preferred to have taken Nan out for a walk and to find somewhere peaceful to break the news, but the recent heavy snow, from the coldest winter in 30 years, had only recently melted.

"I have something to tell you." I said, once we were safely ensconced back in Nan's room away from any eavesdropping or Mrs Caunter's interference.

Nan looked up, I instantly recognised she was expecting bad news.

"Is it Di? Has she gone?"

"No, she's fighting fit. It's Brigitte I'm afraid."

Nan nodded, and looked across to the window sill and the framed photo of Brigitte as a young girl, which Gaby had given to her during our visit last year. I allowed her a few moments of quiet reflection. It is one of the facts of life that once you reach a certain age you are surrounded by death, and unfortunately become familiar with it.

"What was it? Old age?" Nan asked.

"Yes. Very peaceful, she just slipped away one afternoon. Gaby has asked us to come to the funeral."

We had planned to visit Étampes again in July, and in the meantime, Nan had written to Brigitte via Gaby on several occasions, enclosing printouts of old photographs of 1930s Baldock that we had found on the Facebook page. Gaby was enormously grateful for this, and was especially keen that we visit again.

"I can't make the journey in this cold, and to be honest I never find any solace in funerals. You can't see the person you are burying, and you can't have a conversation with them. It just reaffirms that you won't ever see them again. That's why I rarely visit your grandfather's grave. We will pay our respects in another way."

On the day of Brigitte's funeral, a cool but sunny April day, Nan, wrapped up well in several layers, asked me to take her to the Bogs. On our way we purchased some flowers, some red roses, which on our visit to Étampes last summer we had learnt were Brigitte's favourites. The tracks in the Bogs were muddier than I had expected which made it quite difficult to negotiate a route for our planned visit to the highest of the landscaped rubbish tips.

"We should have brought a glass jar with us." I commented.

"No need, there's plenty here. Just ease yourself down that bank, you'll find plenty there. Be careful though!" Nan pointed behind her left shoulder. Sure, enough the remnants of the tip were exposed at the bottom of the slope, intertwined with nettles and other vegetation. Fortunately, I was wearing jeans, so I avoided being stung. Among the collection of mostly broken jars and assorted items of rubbish, I found an unbroken one. Once I had filled it up with water from the River Ivel, I clambered back up the slope and helped Nan arrange the flowers in the jar. After I had placed them on the ground Nan uttered a few words of remembrance.

"Wherever you are, Brigitte, I hope you're safe. I won't ever forget you. We had many good times here. Rest in peace Brigitte."

Gaby has continued to correspond with us both. In her last letter she invited us both to France to visit her again. We still have the remainder of the diaries to read, but I'm not sure Nan is too keen to make the journey, especially now that Brigitte is no longer with us. I shall write to Gaby and invite her to Baldock, so that we can show her around some of the places her mother frequented all those years ago. I think she would like that very much, and I know Nan would be delighted to act as host and guide.

Di is still extremely well for her age and celebrated her 101st birthday last month. Nan will celebrate her 96th birthday next week, so we will all be treated to another cheese feast! She is still going strong, and I have at last persuaded her to share her wartime adventures with the rest of the family. One thing that I have not persuaded her to do is to ease up on subjecting Mrs Caunter to her numerous pranks, though as yet old Bighead still has no idea who the culprit is!